A DARK MAFIA ROMANCE

HEARTS OF THE UNDERWORLD

HEIDI STARK

Sign up for my newsletter for the latest on new releases, promos, giveaways and events!

Join me on social media:
Facebook: @heidistarkauthor
Instagram: @heidistarkauthor
TikTok: @heidistark_author
Twitter: @heidistarkauthr

Website

Interested in joining my team? Apply here:

ARC team

Street team

Marco: Hearts of the Underworld contains several themes that might be triggering for some readers:

- murder

- kidnapping

- graphic violence including torture and mutilation

- graphic sex scenes

- mafia themes

Reader discretion is strongly advised.

This book *does* contain a guaranteed happily ever after.

Dedicated to those who find beauty in the dark, and who
understand that even the coldest heart
can burn bright for the right person.

One

Alessia

T he rising sun spills over the cityscape, bathing the streets in a stunning yet deceiving golden glow. The beauty of the still air belies the darkness lurking in the underbelly of this concrete jungle. Jiggling the door just until I hear the familiar click, I unlock the frosted glass door to La Dolce Vita, my little slice of heaven tucked into the chaos.

The pastel yellow and pink exterior stands out amongst the gray highrises, window boxes overflowing with bursts of crimson and violet. It's been referred to as Instagram-worthy in a plethora of Yelp reviews and Eater articles—not that I personally care about that type of thing very much, although it's fantastic for business.

The aroma of freshly baked cornetti and rich espresso envelops me as I step inside. Not many people get to work in a place that smells this divine. I wave to my lead baker, Ernesto, who has been here since well before the crack of dawn, preparing pastries and confections that will delight customers well into the afternoon. He's a loyal employee, here since it opened, having trained in the same Italian town my family is from. It was nice to be able to give him an opportunity in this part of the world, much like my family received when they moved here decades ago.

Vintage café chairs, painstakingly picked out at countless estate sales and swap meets, sit clustered around metal and wooden tables topped with sugar bowls and miniature vases of vibrant wildflowers. Before long, my baristas shuffle into the café and immediately get to work, and the hiss and gurgle of the espresso machine provides a steady backbeat to the hushed conversations of the few early bird customers. I don't recognize them, but the large backpacks they both wear, and the hoodies emblazoned with the nearby college's sports team logo, are a giveaway they're kicking off their school year.

I tie on my apron, the familiar motions grounding me as I prepare for the day ahead. The oven timer dings in the back, and I help Ernesto to pull out trays of golden, flaky croissants. My heart swells looking around my cozy café. La Dolce Vita isn't much, just a tiny storefront café, but it's mine. A place for comfort, for community, for a little taste of dolce vita in the midst of the churning city. Is this the American Dream that my parents left the old country for, and am I fulfilling their every hope and dream for me? Probably not. I'm sure a café isn't the type of future they envisioned for me. But, at the same time, I'm happy with this little slice of paradise. I bring people joy in their otherwise mundane, chaotic days, after all.

As I top off cups with foamed milk, laughter lines crinkling my eyes, the TV above the counter flickers with a breaking news report on a mob slaying just a few blocks away. A chill runs down my spine, the bubble of my happy place pierced by the creeping fear that has followed my family for generations. Resistant to having a TV in this little sanctuary in the first place, I finally caved in when customers told me it made them feel safer knowing what was taking place on the surrounding blocks. I shake off the dark thoughts, focusing on the people here, on the light we kindle within these walls. Focusing on the safe space I've worked so hard to cultivate. But, even within these walls, the ghosts of the past are never far behind.

I take a deep breath and put on a smile as the door chimes signal the arrival of my first regular.

"Good morning, Mr. Bianchi!" I call out.

The elderly man shuffles in, newspaper tucked under his arm. "Ciao, Alessia," he says in his gravelly voice, beaming at me with his gentle, wise eyes. "The usual for me."

"Coming right up." I pour him a cappuccino, topping it with a sprinkle of cinnamon. As I set it on his table in the corner, I ask, "How are you today?"

"Oh, still breathing," he chuckles. "These old bones aren't what they used to be. They creak and groan so much now every time I move that I'm sure my neighbors are about to make an official noise complaint!"

I laugh softly and pat his shoulder. "Well, you'll always have a seat here. And if your bones get too noisy, we'll just turn the radio up." I wink at him.

He laughs, smiles gratefully and opens his newspaper. I make my way behind the counter just as the door chimes again. A harried young mother comes in, baby bundled against her chest. Her eyes are ringed with exhaustion, but she brightens a bit when she sees me.

"Rough morning, Lucia?" I ask, quirking a brow.

"Gianna has been so fussy," she shakes her head and frowns. "I just needed a minute of peace...and quite a lot of caffeine."

I glance at the sleeping baby and can't help but smile at her innocent wee face. "Looks like she's getting some rest now. Why don't you sit down for a bit? I'll bring you something."

Lucia sighs, tension leaving her body. As I prepare her usual latte, I keep an eye on her as she gently rocks the baby back and forth against her,, Mr. Bianchi's newspaper crinkling in the background as he voraciously devours the latest updates. My heart fills for these people who depend on this haven, on me. No matter what happens in my own life, or what has happened already, I've created this space and I can be a light for them.

I finish up Lucia's drink, adding an extra sprinkle of cinnamon, and bring it over to her.

"Here you go, on the house today."

She looks up, surprised. "Oh Alessia, you don't have to do that."

I wave my hand. "Consider it a gift for the new mama. Enjoy it while she's still asleep." I smile down at Gianna.

Lucia smiles, grasping the warm cup. "You're too kind. I don't know what I'd do without this place."

I give her shoulder a gentle squeeze before moving back behind the counter. As I tidy up, the morning sun streams in through the front windows, catching the various vintage mirrors and framed photos on the walls. It gives the café a warm, nostalgic glow, like a faded photograph from generations past.

I pause to glance at my reflection in the mirror behind the counter. My dark hair is swept up in its usual loose bun, soft tendrils curling around my face. The corner of my mouth quirks up as I notice a smudge of flour on my cheek from this morning's baking. I wipe it away, smoothing down my plum colored apron. A glint catches my eye—the delicate gold locket resting at the base of my throat. I grasp it briefly, taking a small measure of comfort from its familiar weight.

The bell chimes again, pulling me from my reverie. I turn to greet the new customers with a bright smile, pushing away the shadows, if only for a moment. This café, these people—they are my purpose. The rent may be rising with what feels like every passing day, and crime rates may be shooting up at lightning speed, but this place matters to a whole bunch of people, and I will protect our small haven of light for as long as I can.

I take a deep breath, inhaling the rich aroma of the coffee beans, freshly ground and brewing. This place truly is my sanctuary. From the moment I opened La Dolce Vita's doors, I found joy in creating a space that felt like home. Over the years, I've come to know the regulars well. Mrs. Alvarez, who sits by the window with her crossword puzzles. Tom, the accountant who rushes in every morning for his double espresso before work. Gemma, whose baby girl took her first steps here. They're like family.

My gaze lands on the old black and white photograph hanging on the far wall—the one of my great grandparents standing proudly outside their neighborhood bakery. La Dolce Vita carries on their legacy. But I can't help but feel, although I can't put my finger on why exactly, it comes with darker echoes from the past.

The bell over the door rings, jolting me from my thoughts. I glance up to see two men enter the café, their expensive suits and hard expressions out of place among the students, young professionals and elderly customers. A chill runs down my spine as I meet the cold, assessing gaze of the taller man. His eyes remind me too much of my father's—ruthless and unforgiving.

They take a seat in the back corner, speaking in hushed tones. I fight the unease twisting in my gut. This is my haven, I remind myself. But I can't escape the feeling that the shadows have found me at last. The ghosts of my family are not so easily outrun.

Two

Marco

The dim light casts ominous shadows across the dark wood walls of my office. I sit behind an imposing mahogany desk, my posture rigid, exuding complete authority. My tailored three-piece suit fits like a glove, crisp white shirt immaculate, my cufflinks glinting in the low light. There's not a paper out of place on the vast desktop. I fold my hands, my gaze intense, piercing. This is my domain. My empire.

I built this from nothing. Clawed my way up from the gutter through grit and ruthlessness. Now I rule this city's underbelly with an iron fist. None dare challenge me, not even my most hardened rivals. The old dons scoffed at me once. Not anymore.

A knock at the door. "Enter," I bark out. My capo, Luca, slinks in. The man glances around nervously despite our years together. Good. He still fears me.

"The shipment arrived at the docks, boss." Luca licks his lips anxiously. "But we got a problem..."

My eyes narrow, jaw tightening. "Explain." My tone brooks no argument. Luca flinches. He knows how I feel about problems.

"The Irish...they hit our warehouse last night. Took the whole stash."

Rage courses through me. "And you let this happen?" My voice drops to a deadly whisper.

Luca pales. "It was the O'Malleys, boss. We was outnumbered—"

"How did they know which warehouse we were using? We just changed locations."

"We're looking into it, boss."

"And they took everything? Weren't we securing product in multiple batches to avoid this?"

"Yeah, we don't know how they knew. Like I said, we're looking into it... but there were just so many of them—"

I slam my fist on the desk. Luca jumps. "No excuses!" I snap. "I gave you one task. Secure the product."

I take a breath, steadying myself. "The Irish will pay for this insult." I meet Luca's eyes. "As will you."

He gulps, nodding quickly. Message received. I do not tolerate failure.

I wave Luca away in dismissal and lean back, contemplating my next move. The O'Malleys will learn what happens when they cross me. They might be scrappy and resourceful, but I built this empire through ruthlessness and sheer force of will. And I'll be damned if I let some upstart Irish punks take what's mine.

I have no illusions that things will just continue along like they have been for so many years. The city still belongs to me. For now, at least. But the shadows are shifting, strange tidings reaching my ear. Change is coming. I can feel it. And I must be ready.

I steeple my fingers, contemplating the news Luca delivered. The Irish stealing our shipment is a bold move, one that cannot go unanswered. But retaliation requires careful calculation. I cannot be rash, despite the rage burning inside me. Rashness costs money, costs lives. And I can't afford to lose either right now.

I press a button on my desk. "Send in Aldo."

Moments later, my trusted advisor enters. Aldo's face is lined with years of service. He bows respectfully. "You summoned me, boss?"

" The Irish hit our warehouse. Took everything."

Aldo's expression darkens. "The O'Malleys? Those snakes. What are your orders?"

I tap my fingers on the desk. "Ready our men. But do not act yet. I want to know how the Irish knew about the shipment, who their informant is." My eyes bore into Aldo's. "Find the rat, then we make our move."

He nods. "I'll take care of it personally."

"Good. This insult will not stand." I dismiss Aldo, knowing that if anyone can track down a rat, it's him, and turn my chair to gaze out the window overlooking the city, bathed in evening light. From up here, everything seems orderly, tranquil. But I know the truth. The city seethes with unseen rivalries, constantly threatening to boil over.

Maintaining power requires eternal vigilance. Enemies lurk in every shadow, everyone posturing and positioning to make a power grab. To take what's mine. I trust no one, rely on no one. It's a lonely perch, but one I must occupy alone.

I close my eyes, allowing myself a moment of vulnerability. But only a moment. Sentiment is a luxury I cannot afford, and certainly a weakness I have no place displaying in front of my men. With a deep breath, I steel myself once more, squaring my shoulders.

The city awaits my response. And respond I shall.

The sun sets over the city, casting long shadows over the gleaming skyscrapers. On the bustling streets below, crowds of workers pour out of offices, eager to start their weekend. Bright lights flicker on, neon signs and gaudy billboards advertising trendy restaurants and clubs.

But in my office high above, I brood in solitude, the lively city nothing but a distant backdrop. This is the price of power—isolation, separation.

My phone buzzes. "Boss, I was able to confirm it. The Irish have completely cleared out the warehouse. Over two million in product, gone." Aldo's gravelly voice is strained.

I suppress a flare of anger. "Then it's time we return the favor. Hit their fronts in the south side tonight. All of them."

"With pleasure." A hint of anticipation in Aldo's reply. "We'll teach those nervy bastards a lesson."

I end the call, turning back to the window. Far below, crowds of oblivious revelers flock to restaurants, bars and nightclubs, seeking escape and entertainment. A world away from mine, yet still under my unseen influence. They have no idea of the strings I pull behind the scenes, how much I impact their daily lives without them having the slightest inkling.

In a dingy bar downtown, I imagine a greasy man in a trenchcoat is handing a fat envelope to a steely-eyed Irish enforcer. Payment for services rendered. The rat who sold us out.

In an abandoned lot, I know my men are unloading cans of gasoline and materials for makeshift explosives, preparing for tonight's job. I can almost feel the furtive glances into the shadows, everyone on edge.

I glance at my surveillance cameras. A young couple kisses in a corner booth at one of my jazz clubs, as my men sweep the room, keeping close watch on a city councilman in my pocket. Nothing can disrupt his crucial vote next week.

The city lives and breathes according to my silent machinations, even as ordinary citizens remain unaware. This is the power—and the burden—of my position. I rule an empire hidden in plain sight, obeyed yet unseen. I call the shots, but never take them myself. There's a power in my understated silence, but sometimes I have to fight the urge to yell from the rooftops, to destroy threats with my own bare hands.

For now, the smooth facade of the city remains intact. But trouble brews beneath. My clash with the Irish is only the beginning. Other threats loom, both within and without. I must be ready.

The city depends on it.

I lean back in my leather chair, gazing out at the city lights stretching into the distance. Another long night ahead, and always more work to be done.

My desk is immaculately organized, files and reports perfectly aligned. Not a pen out of place. I appreciate order, discipline, control. The same principles applied to my business.

A knock at the door interrupts my thoughts. "Come in," I call out, my voice steady and commanding

Two of my other captains enter, their postures rigid with tension. Ricci and Morales. Loyal soldiers who have bled for me before and who wouldn't hesitate to again. I gesture for them to sit.

"The Irish aren't letting this go," Ricci begins without preamble. "They hit our warehouse in the docks tonight. Torched the whole damn thing."

I nod calmly. On reflection, I expected some form of retaliation given we've been honing in on their territory. Plus, of course, I've already heard about this from both Luca and Aldo. I'm still undecided about whether to be flattered or perturbed that my capos are bringing time-sensitive updates directly to me without conferring with each other first. "And our merchandise?"

"Salvaged most of it in time," Morales replies. "But they sent a message, boss. Took out two of our guys in the process."

My jaw tightens almost imperceptibly. "Who?"

"Safton and Trujillo." He looks down.

Damn. Two good men lost, and resources destroyed. Families now without fathers. Unacceptable.

"I know it was the O'Malleys, but... any leads on who sanctioned the hit?" I ask. We must know the source before striking back. No rash decisions.

The men exchange a look. "Word is it came from the top. Finn himself."

Finn O'Malley. The Irish kingpin who fancies himself my rival. A brazen move, even for him. The time has come to remind him exactly with whom he is dealing.

"Set up a meet with Finn's crew," I order decisively. "He wants a war? We'll bring him one."

My captains nod, accustomed to my swift action. Indecision is poison in this business.

"And the warehouse?" Ricci asks.

"Torch one of his in return. Send a crew tonight. I think Luca's already getting everyone organized."

Ricci's eyes widen at the mention of Luca, and that clearly this isn't the first time I'd heard about the O'Malley's attack. "With respect, boss, that may only escalate things further—"

I silence Ricci's protest with a raised hand. "I will not permit this insult to go unanswered. Finn must learn his place."

My word is final. Ricci bows his head in acquiescence, and Morales nods.

They know our code, I have proven myself a leader who commands respect, but who is not be crossed. Finn will come to understand this too...one way or another. To remain silent and allow anything other than swift retaliation would be to concede, to wave a white flag and surrender the turf we've fought tirelessly to accumulate.

I dismiss my men to carry out their tasks. As the door closes behind them, the weight of leadership settles on my shoulders once more. I crave no war, only stability. But order must be maintained, even if by force.

This is the burden I bear for those under my command. And bear it I shall, whatever the cost.

Alone again in my office, I pour myself two fingers of Scotch and sink into the leather armchair by the window. The day's events weigh heavy on my mind.

My gaze falls on the framed photo on my desk—-the only personal effect in this stark, imposing space. It's a photo of Mr. Bianchi, my mentor, the man who plucked me off the streets and taught me everything. He saw potential in me when no one else did.

I swallow hard against the lump in my throat as I remember the day he was gunned down. It was the only time I've ever seen Giancarlo Bianchi afraid. He shielded me with his body as the bullets flew. I still remember the wet warmth of his blood soaking my shirt as he took his last breath.

Losing him devastated me. He was the closest thing I had to the idea of a father. In that moment, the last scraps of innocence died within me. From then on, my heart turned to stone. I vowed I would never again let someone get close enough to hurt me that deeply.

And so I've entombed myself in this fortress of solitude, surrounding myself with money, power, and pretty women, yet letting none of them past my defenses. I've become untouchable, unbreakable.

But there are times, like now, when the silence weighs oppressively, reminding me of all I've given up in exchange for control and security. Times when Bianchi's smiling face cuts through the darkness, leaving an aching void behind. What would he say if he saw me now? Would he be proud, or would he caution me against shutting myself off completely?

With a weary sigh, I swallow the scotch in one burning gulp. The war for the streets goes on, but inside, a part of me remains that lost boy mourning his fallen mentor. My empire flourishes, yet I've never felt more alone.

I stand and move to the window, gazing out at the city lights twinkling below. This is all mine, though few know the extent of my reach. From the penthouses to the projects, everyone pays their dues, whether in money, loyalty, or blood.

But lately, rumblings of unrest have begun to stir. Old rivalries threaten to ignite again, of which there is no shortage. And there are whispers of an ambitious newcomer looking to stake his claim.

Change is coming. I can sense it as surely as I can feel the cold glass beneath my fingertips. The underworld is like a slumbering beast—volatile, hangry, and quick to bite when provoked.

But I'm part of that underworld—an important part—and I've worked too hard for too long to lose my hold now. If it's a war they want, I'll bring hell's fury down upon them. I've survived this long by being cunning, ruthless, and always staying one step ahead. Let them come at me with their pathetic plots. Burn one of my warehouses down? I'll burn down three of yours and sell your daughter into sex trafficking after letting all my guys test her out first. Try me. They have no idea who they're dealing with.

I turn from the window, energy coiling tightly in my muscles. My time for brooding is over. There are calls to be made, orders to give. Wheels must be set in motion to consolidate power before the tides can shift against me.

The city holds its breath, blissfully unaware of the chaos about to be unleashed. And I will be the eye of the storm—unflinching, uncompromising. For in the end, only the strongest survive. The streets have taught me that much.

My reflection is interrupted by a knock at the door.

"Enter," I call out, my voice low but commanding.

Luca steps back into the office. I study him closely. His face is grim, his eyes troubled. But I get the sense he hasn't just come to give me a recap on our earlier discussion about the O'Malleys and the attack on the warehouse. Something else is wrong.

"What is it?" I ask, skipping the niceties.

Luca hesitates before answering. "It's about the property on 5th and Pine. There's been a...complication."

I feel my body tense. The building on 5th is a key strategic holding, critical for expanding my reach downtown. I had planned to acquire it quietly through various shell companies.

"What kind of complication?" I press.

"The owner backed out of the sale at the last minute. Refused to sign the papers."

My eyes narrow. This makes no sense. The owner is deep in debt, desperate for a way out. My people had made him an offer too lucrative to pass up. Or so it had seemed.

"Why?" I ask sharply.

Luca shifted on his feet. "He said something about getting a better deal. From who, we don't know yet."

I consider this new information, my mind racing through the possibilities. A better offer only means one thing—someone else has gotten to the owner first. Which implies they've caught wind of my plans.

An unsettling thought, particularly when it seems like someone had inside information about one of our warehouses, too.

I think of the whispers I've been hearing, rumblings of a new faction angling for power. Is this their opening gambit? A warning shot across the bow? If so, they have no grasp of the beast they've just provoked. Or is it the stirring of old rivalries, no more than a seasonal jostling for position near the boundaries of our respective turf?

I meet Luca's anxious gaze. "Find out everything you can about this new buyer. I want a name by nightfall."

Luca nods. As he turns to leave, I add quietly, "And Luca...dig deep. We need to know exactly who we're dealing with."

The door closes, leaving me alone again in the shadows. A slow smile spreads across my face, devoid of warmth or humor. Let them come at me from the darkness, whoever they may be. They'll soon learn that I still reign supreme in this city. And my rivals always have a way of disappearing without a trace...

Three

Alessia

The aroma of freshly brewed coffee surrounds me as I unlock the front door of the café and step inside. Morning light filters through the windows, washing the room in a warm glow. Ernesto has baked treats to last the day, and is off delivering breads and pastries to local restaurants. This is my favorite time of day, before the sign on the door is turned around to signal we're open, when it's just me and the tranquil quiet.

I go through my opening routine, brewing a fresh pot of dark roast, arranging the pastries in the glass case just so. As I water the potted plants by the window, I can already picture my regulars filtering in—Mrs. Chen with her crossword puzzle, Jamal on his way to class. Their faces are as familiar as family, their stories taking up places in my heart. Provide someone with exceptional hospitality, and you'd be surprised at what they're willing and eager to share with you.

The bells jingle merrily as I flip the sign to 'Open.' Right on cue, Mrs. Chen shuffles in, making a beeline for her usual table.

"Morning, Alessia dear," she says. "Can I get my usual?"

"Of course, Mrs. Chen." I pour her a cup of coffee just the way she likes it, with just a splash of cream.

As I deliver it to her table, she pats my hand affectionately. "You make the best coffee in town, sweetie."

I smile, warmth blooming in my chest. This is why I open the café every morning, for moments like this—the community that gathers here, the bonds between us. Though it's a simple living, there's joy to be found in the smallest of things.

I'm wiping down the front counter when Jamal comes bounding in, backpack slung over one shoulder.

"Morning, Miss Alessia!" he says brightly, leaning against the counter. His eyes light up as he surveys the variety of pastries in the display case, although I already know what he's going to order. "The usual breakfast sandwich and coffee to go, please."

I grin and gesture to show him I've already started preparing his order. "Someone's chipper this morning. Ready for that big test today?"

"You remembered!" He says, his face lighting up. "And you bet I'm ready!" He taps his knuckles against the counter. "I've been studying all week. I got thi—"

He stops abruptly, his gaze fixed out the front window behind me. I glance over my shoulder to see what's caught his attention.

There's a sleek black sedan idling across the street, windows tinted. Something about it raises the hairs on the back of my neck. As I stare, two more pull up along the curb, cutting off a bus trying to pull into its stop.

My stomach drops. I don't recognize these cars. They don't belong in my neighborhood.

I turn back to Jamal, who's frowning deeply. "What's going on out there, Miss Alessia?" he asks nervously. "I've never seen those cars around here before."

I wish I had an answer for him. My unease grows as I notice a group of men loitering down the block, watching the café. They're dressed in fine suits—so out of place for this part of town. Yet they're dressed similarly to the two men who were in here the other day. I usually have a knack for faces, but their appearance is just so... cookie cutter... that I couldn't tell you if they were in fact the same guys.

"I'm not sure," I reply slowly. I hand Jamal his sandwich and coffee. "Maybe you should head to school a different way today, okay? Why don't you head out the back through the kitchen, and help yourself to a sfogliatelle on your way."

He nods, eyes wide. "Yeah, good idea. Thank you for the pastry! See you tomorrow, Miss Alessia "

As he hurries out through the back, I can't shake the ominous feeling settling over me. Something isn't right.

Mrs. Chen glances up from her crossword, brow furrowed. "Strange folks hanging around outside today," she remarks, gesturing in the direction of the suited men. "Gives me the heebie-jeebies."

I just nod grimly, goosebumps spreading across my arms and causing me to shiver. I have a bad feeling about this.

The bell above the door jingles as it's thrown open, the cheerful sound at odds with the imposing figure that strides in.

He's tall, well over six feet, with a muscular frame shown off by his tailored suit. His hair is black, cropped short on the sides but longer on top, where it's slicked back from his face. High cheekbones and a strong jawline give him an aristocratic handsomeness, but it's the intensity of his icy blue eyes that makes him truly striking.

Those piercing eyes sweep the interior of my café, seeming to miss nothing. I feel pinned in place as they settle on me for a long moment before moving on.

My heart is racing and my mouth goes dry. Everything about this man screams danger, from the coiled tension in his powerful body to the subtle air of command that surrounds him. He moves with the relaxed grace of a predator.

But as unsettled as I am by his presence, I can't ignore the involuntary attraction I feel either. He's possibly the most gorgeous man I've ever seen. There's a magnetic pull to him that's impossible to resist, despite the undercurrent of menace he carries. And maybe because of it.

He heads straight for the counter, the other patrons shrinking back instinctively to clear a path. When he reaches me, he leans in, hands braced on the worn wood. His scent envelops me, clean and masculine.

"I need to speak with you," he says, his voice a low rumble that sends heat curling through me. "Now."

My mouth goes dry again under the intensity of that glacier gaze. I have no idea who this dangerous stranger is, but I know with sudden certainty that my life will never be the same.

I steel myself and meet his intense gaze head-on. "I'm listening," I say evenly, hoping he doesn't notice the slight tremor in my hands. "Can I get you something? A coffee or a pastry, maybe?" I gesture at the counter in front of him.

His eyes narrow, likely unused to being challenged. "Not here. Somewhere private."

I bristle at his presumption. "Anything you want to discuss with me can be said right here."

He steps closer, using his impressive height to loom over me. "I don't think you want your customers hearing this conversation," he says, voice pitched low.

I glance around quickly, noting the avid interest on the nearby faces. He's right, the last thing I need is to alarm my regulars.

"Fine," I bite out. "We can talk in the back office, five minutes." I'm taking a risk, but something tells me he won't take no for an answer.

He gives a curt nod and moves away. Beckoning one of my baristas over to man the cash register, I head to the office on shaky legs, berating myself. I should call the police, not entertain this threatening stranger. But he hasn't exactly done anything wrong yet, and something tells me the police would be useless against him anyway.

I just need to hear him out, then send him on his way. Maybe sneak a few peeks at his handsome face and his ripped body that ripples underneath his suit. I can handle five minutes alone with him. I think.

I take a deep breath to steady my nerves before entering the office, closing the door behind me. He stands with his back to me, perusing the café photos on my wall. He cuts an imposing figure even from behind, tall and broad-shouldered in an impeccably tailored suit that makes me think about nothing more than what his body looks like underneath. Tattoos peek out from under his shirt cuffs and his shirt collar. Neck *and* hand tattoos, my God.

I clear my throat and he turns, pinning me with an assessing look. "Well?" I ask tightly "Who are you, for starters? And what's so important you had to disrupt my business?"

His mouth quirks. "Straight to the point. I appreciate that." He moves closer and I fight the urge to step back. "I have some business nearby that requires discretion. I don't want any...interference. I'm Marco De Luca. You may have heard of me."

My eyes widen as his meaning and the weight of his last name both sink in. But something inside tells me to play it cool. "Doesn't ring a bell."

He eyes me with skepticism. "You really have no idea?"

"Look, all I know is you've come in here and demanded I speak with you right during one of the busiest parts of my day. My customers count on me, you know? Do you know how many conflicts are resolved through adequately caffeinating people? By giving them a sweet treat so flaky and buttery that the only things that come out of their mouths are productive and positive?"

He smirks. "That's all very cute, but that's not the part of your business that I'm interested in."

I sigh. "Criminal business. That's what you're talking about." The conversation, and his presence, are making me uneasy. But my attempts to deflect the subject to more comfortable territory clearly aren't working, so I may as well cut to the chase.

"Labels," he says dismissively. "The point is, it would be best for all involved if your café wasn't operating for a few weeks."

My eyes grow wide. "Excuse me? You're asking me to just... shut my business down? No reason. Just as simple as that?"

"Precisely," Marco nods.

My temper flares. "That's not going to happen. This is my livelihood, and my regulars rely on me to provide coffee and a safe space. I won't let you drive me out."

His eyes flash with surprise and something like amusement. "You don't seem to understand your position here."

"No, you don't understand," I fire back. "I've worked too hard to build this café. Your actions won't control my life."

He considers me silently. Then he steps even closer, forcing me to tilt my head back to meet his eyes. "You're either very brave or very foolish," he murmurs.

My breath catches at his proximity but I lift my chin. "I protect what's mine. That includes my café, my community, my freedom to live without fear. If you try to take that from me, you'll regret it. And while we're on the topic, you and your men need to stop coming around here—to this neighborhood, and to this cafe. You're scaring my customers."

For a long moment we're locked in a battle of wills, the air simmering between us. Then I see a flicker of respect in his eyes. Without a word, he turns and leaves. The outer door slams behind him.

I sag against the wall, my adrenaline draining away. I don't know if I've won this round, but I have a strong feeling that my clash with Marco's underworld has only just begun. Men like him don't give up that easily. In fact, from what I've heard sometimes they don't give up at all.

I take a shaky breath, trying to calm my racing heart as I watch Marco's imposing figure disappear down the street. Our heated confrontation replays in my mind—his cool arrogance, the implicit threats, and my own defiant stance against him. Did I go too far? Did I put my cafe and my employees and customers at risk by not just caving to his unreasonable demands? The audacity. Asking me to just shut down my business for a few weeks with no reason given. Who does he think he is?

I've never met someone who exudes such raw power and danger. Yet part of me thrilled in that exchange, drawn to the intensity in his stormy eyes. Marco awakened something primal in me, a recklessness I've never felt before.

But I know he also represents everything I stand against. His world of crime and violence is an affront to the community I've built here. I won't let him poison this neighborhood for his own gain, as has happened to so many communities in adjacent districts.

Still, as I wipe down the counter with shaking hands, I can't ignore the swooping sensation in my stomach when I recall his closeness. The memory of his breath on my cheek, his imposing strength barely leashed. My mind is spinning from our interaction. I've never met someone who affected me so viscerally—his sheer presence was like a lightning storm sweeping through my peaceful little cafe.

I think back to the smoldering intensity of his gaze, the coiled strength in his muscular frame barely leashed as he leaned toward me. I feel my cheeks flush as I recall his breath grazing my skin, the heady scent of his cologne enveloping me.

There's an undeniable magnetism to Marco that both unsettles and excites me. But I also know he represents everything I've tried to build a shelter against—the violence, greed and cruelty of his underworld domain. I have a feeling this first clash is only the beginning. That there are dangerous days ahead.

But while I might seem timid, a small business owner who makes pretty and fluffy pastries and drinks for people, that exterior belies the steel I have buried deep inside. If Marco wants a fight, I'll give him one. If Marco thinks he could intimidate me into compromising my values, he's mistaken.

Because what he doesn't know about me is I'll give as good as I get, particuarly when people I care about are threatened. And I won't, can't, let him corrupt this neighborhood I've poured my heart into. My cafe is a sanctuary—not just for me but for others, especially for those trying to escape the shadows Marco and men like him have cast across the city. I've seen the bruises, the hunched shoulders, the hunted and haunted eyes of those seeking refuge within these walls.

I steel my resolve, even as an unwelcome thrill courses through me at the memory of Marco's powerful presence. Our first clash felt like it was only the beginning. With a man of his status, I can only imagine there will be more storms ahead, dangerous tempests of Marco's making. I shiver, uncomfortable with the interest he's taken in my cafe. And if he's interested in it, maybe so are other people who aren't so... incredibly attractive or polite.

I take a deep breath as I wipe down the cafe counter, trying to steady my rattled nerves after Marco's abrupt departure. The memory of his icy blue eyes and imposing presence still linger, sending an involuntary shiver through me. I know with uneasy certainty that my clash with Marco was only the first gust of the storm to come. His business, whatever its nature, is more than likely going to keep encroaching on my neighborhood. And I sense that Marco isn't a man who tolerates defiance for long.

There will be consequences for my show of resistance, I have no doubt of that. Men like him don't mess around, and violence—or even death—are not off the table. But I now understand I have reserves of strength I've never had to call upon before. When Marco returns—because I have no doubt he will—I'll be ready. I will do everything in my power to protect this community, this little island of light amidst gathering shadows.

Come what may, I refuse to retreat or yield to Marco's agenda. He has awoken something defiant and unbreakable within me. A fierce desire to protect what's mine and the people I care about. Let him come at me with the full fury of his underworld might; I'll show Marco what true strength looks like. My cafe, my community, are worth fighting for.

Four

Alessia

I'm digging through my storage room, clearing out old boxes and clutter that have accumulated over the years. As I shift a heavy crate, a faded envelope flutters out. Curious, I pick it up and peel back the brittle seal. Inside is a black-and-white photograph of a young couple, their arms wrapped around each other, all smiles and laughter.

I don't recognize them at first, but as I study the woman's face, so similar to photos I've seen of my mother when she was younger, it hits me—this is a photo of my parents. But why was it stashed away, hidden from sight all these years?

My mind races as I examine the photo closely, taking in every detail. My parents look so carefree, so in love. Not at all like the solemn, burdened people I knew growing up. What happened to them? There's a date scrawled on the back—two years before I was born.

What don't I know about my family's past? About my parents' lives before me? I thought our world was always the family bakery and other hospitality enterprises, our family bound by routine and stability. But now questions swell inside me, breaking open the history I thought I knew.

There must be more photos, letters—clues about my family's hidden stories. I have to learn the truth. Gripping the photo tightly, I head upstairs, determined to search the above-cafe apartment from top to bottom. My parents' room. There must be answers there about who they were before responsibility and expectation weighed them down. Before I became their family burden, inheritor of secrets I'm now desperate to unveil. But first, there's something I have to do.

I take a deep breath before knocking on the door to my grandmother's room, the photo clutched in my sweaty palm.

"Nonna Giulia? Can I come in?" My voice wavers slightly.

"Of course, dear."

I enter slowly. My grandmother sits in her favorite armchair, glasses perched on her nose as she reviews the cafe's books. I hover in the doorway, suddenly unsure.

"What is it, Alessia?" She peers at me over her glasses.

"I...I found this." I hold out the photo with trembling fingers. "Why was it hidden away?"

My grandmother's normally stoic face pales at the sight of it. She lays the books aside and beckons me over. I perch on the tufted ottoman, facing her.

"It's time you learned the truth about our family's past, Alessia. I never wanted to burden you with it, but I knew deep down that this day would inevitably come." She takes a shaky breath. "The Moretti name has a dark history, tied to the mafia. Your parents tried to break free from that world, but the ties were too deep. They—and later, I—spent years shielding you from it, hoping it would never chase you like it chased them."

I gasp, reeling in disbelief. Our family? Part of the mafia? It can't be real. We've always lived such a simple, quiet life doing simple work... at least, that's what I was led to believe. I saw it with my own eyes, participated in the modest existence of a family who lives to serve others. But my grandmother's somber eyes don't waver.

"No." I feel the color drain from my own face. "How could you keep this from me?" I search her expression frantically, trying to reconcile my peaceful world with this shocking legacy lurking beneath the surface.

My grandmother reaches for my hand, her own still trembling. "I only wanted to protect you, Alessia. To give you the innocent childhood your parents never had."

I sit in stunned silence, the photo fluttering from my grasp. My identity, my past—suddenly strange and laced with menace. What else have they kept from me? I must learn the truth, no matter how dark. The Moretti name has marked me, despite all their efforts. But this is all new to me, and I feel far from equipped to deal with this information. Both in light of the threats it represents, but also what it means for my identity. Who even am I anymore?

Giulia's eyes glisten with tears as she continues.

"Your parents were not violent people, Alessia. But the mafia's reach is long, its roots run deep. As a girl, your mother was groomed to marry the son of a powerful mafia boss, sealing an alliance between the families."

I shudder, imagining my gentle mother trapped in that world.

"The marriage was arranged when she was just a child. By the time she came of age, she wanted no part of it. Your father helped her escape to America, away from the endless cycle of violence and obligation. But they could never fully break free."

Giulia pauses, lost in the past. I prompt her gently. "What happened then, Nonna?"

She refocuses on me with a sad smile. "Even an ocean away, the mafia never forgets a debt. Your parents were forced into money laundering to repay what was seen as a betrayal. It was the only way to protect you."

I feel sick at the thought of my parents' predicament. Ensnared by a past they didn't choose, compromising their values for my safety. It's a heavy inheritance. Then, spending their time on trying to protect me from the realities of what I'd been born into... but for what? They both died much before their time, leaving me an orphan. Was it all worth it in the end?

"The mafia world is patient. They bid their time with your parents, believing you could still be...useful. As the last Moretti heir, obligations remain." Giulia grips my hand tightly. "You must be vigilant, principessa."

My breath catches. The café, my home—nowhere is safe from this insidious web. I'm haunted by a legacy I never asked for. But I will not surrender to it. I am still my parents' daughter, and no matter what they were involved in before I was born, they were both good people. That must count for something.

I stare out the café window, watching people pass by on the bustling street outside. They all look so blissfully unaware, going about their normal lives. I envy their ignorance. Or maybe their lives harbor even more dark secrets than my own, but they have yet to find out about it.

Just yesterday, I was one of them. Now a heavy darkness surrounds me, changing everything I thought I knew.

I turn back to Giulia. "How could Mamma and Papa keep this from me? Didn't I deserve to know the truth?"

Giulia sighs, her eyes full of sympathy. "They wanted to shield you for as long as possible. To avoid you growing up like they did... knowing nothing other than the cage they felt they'd been brought into. When you were born, it was like a fresh start—a chance to break from the past."

I shake my head bitterly. "But the past found me anyway."

"Si, principessa." She sighs. "I know it's a terrible burden to bear."

My mind races with questions. Have I been unknowingly helping the mafia all this time, letting them launder money through the café? Are we still indebted to them? How far will they go to collect?

I think of Marco De Luca and his interest in utilizing the café for some strategic purpose. Wanting me to shut it down for weeks so he could do some type of business transaction. Is it all just a front to bring me deeper into their world?

Fear courses through me. I don't want this. But defying the mafia comes with a steep price. My parents paid it with their lives.

Giulia seems to read my thoughts. She cups my face gently. "Whatever comes, remember who you are. The legacy in your heart, not your blood."

I close my eyes, drawing strength from her words. She's right—I can't let this corrupt my spirit. I'm still Alessia Moretti, cafe owner and orphan, and I control my destiny.

But at the same time, what does this mean in terms of who I am? The shadows of the past are lurking, but it's a past I didn't know existed until now.

I take a deep breath and open my eyes, meeting Giulia's worried gaze. She looks so frail now, the weight of years and sorrow etched into her face. I realize with a pang that I can't burden her any further with my fears. This is my cross to bear.

"Thank you for telling me the truth, Nonna Giulia," I say, squeezing her hand. "I know it wasn't easy."

Giulia nods, blinking back tears. "I'll always be here if you need me. But you're strong, Alessia. Stronger than you know."

I manage a small smile, hoping she's right. We hold each other for a long moment, drawing comfort from the embrace.

Then the bell on the café door chimes, breaking the spell. I pull back and smooth my apron, composing myself before I greet the customer.

But when I turn, my blood runs cold. Marco De Luca saunters in, flanked by two hulking men in sharp suits. The café is empty—we're closed, save for Giulia and I tidying up.

Marco's ice-blue eyes spear me as his lips twist into a knowing smirk.

"Buonasera, principessa," he purrs. "I was in the neighborhood and thought I'd stop by to...chat."

My heart hammers. I fight to keep my voice steady. "I'm afraid we're closed for the day. You'll have to come back tomorrow."

Marco tsks, wandering closer. "Come now, we have important business to discuss. Family business."

I clench my fists, standing my ground. The shadows press in, but I will not falter. Not this time. The past will not claim me so easily.

I hold Marco's icy gaze, refusing to be intimidated.

There's a sound of shuffling, and Nonna appears in the doorframe, leaning against it to prop up her spindly frame.

"I don't know what you want, but you need to leave," I say firmly. "We have nothing to discuss."

Marco clicks his tongue. "Such fire. I can see why Dante was so taken with your mother. She had the same spirit."

I bristle at the mention of my late parents, but bite my tongue. Marco is clearly trying to provoke me.

"Don't speak of my family," I snap. "You know nothing about them."

"Oh, but I do," Marco purrs, stepping closer until I can smell his cologne. I want to call it cloying, but if I'm honest it's intoxicating, intriguing... perfect for him. He glances toward Nonna Giulia and nods. "Your nonna told you all about your family's past, didn't she? About their ties to la costa nostra." His timing is impeccable. My eyes flit around the room. Has he got this place bugged? More likely a coincidence, but I wouldn't put it past him.

I clench my fists. Giulia watches silently, fear and something else in her eyes.

Marco leans in, his breath hot on my ear. "You can't run from this, principessa. It's in your blood."

Rage boils up in me. I glance over at Nonna, and she almost imperceptibly shakes her head, as if she knows what's coming even before I do. Before I can think, I slap Marco hard across the face. The crack echoes in the empty cafe.

"Get out," I hiss through gritted teeth.

Marco's cheek reddens where I struck him. For a moment, his cool façade cracks, fury blazing in his eyes. His jaw twitches. Then, just as quickly, he recovers, smoothing his suit jacket.

"You'll regret that, tesoro," he says softly. "This isn't over."

He turns on his heel and stalks out, flanked by his men. The door slams behind them with an ominous finality.

I let out a shaky breath, my false bravado melting away. My eyes meet Nonna's. What have I gotten myself into? What have I gotten us into?

Five

Marco

I sit at my desk, staring at the blank wall as if it holds the answers I seek. But there are no easy solutions here. Only impossible choices between shades of gray.

I've always lived by a code—keep your head down, handle problems in-house, and protect your own. It's how things work in this world. But Alessia Moretti doesn't belong to my world. She's an innocent, even if her family ties run deep in the underground. She didn't even find out until the other day, that much was clear from the way she looked at me in the cafe. And now those ties have put her directly in the crosshairs. With the tension in the city at an all-time high, she's unknowingly become part of a powder keg that's about to explode.

I rub my temples, feeling the onset of a headache. Ever since I learned she's been marked, I haven't been able to get her out of my head. Maybe it's the echo of her laughter from that day at the cafe, so free and full of life. Or the fire in her eyes when we argued over nothing. Here I am, one of the most powerful men in the city, and this little firecracker slapped me right across the face. She refused to shut her cafe down for me. There's a spirit in her that's rare in this weary city. But it's not enough. If I stand by and do nothing, the darkness will swallow her whole.

The timing was incredible. For business reasons, I do need to utilize a space in the same vicinity of her cafe. But to find out her family's debt has been resurrected by a neighboring family in the same week? Almost unbelievable, but sometimes life is mysterious like that.

Is it my problem to solve? No. I owe that girl nothing. But the thought of her warm light being snuffed out by my world makes my gut twist. I don't know what it is about her, but from the moment I met her, I had an insatiable urge to protect her. She doesn't deserve this burden—it's one she never asked for.

I'm surprised by my reaction to her. It's not like we've spent any real time together... for the most part, I've just admired her from afar. But at this rate, if I were to take her on a date, I might be open to burning the world down if she asked me to.

I glance at the photo on my desk, my only reminder of the man who taught me everything. "You would know what to do," I whisper. But he's gone, and the choice falls to me.

With a heavy sigh, I make my decision. Right or wrong, I can't watch her become another casualty, not when I have the power to intervene. I push away from the desk and grab my coat. There are risks, but I will face them.

Some debts transcend family ties and codes of conduct. Protecting her is simply the right thing to do. I only hope she will understand why this must be done.

My black sedan glides to a stop outside Alessia's cafe, the tempting smell of espresso and sugar wafting through the open door. I step out into the golden afternoon light, bracing myself. This won't be easy, but it's necessary.

Inside, Alessia stands behind the counter, laughing with a customer, effortlessly beautiful as always. Her wavy dark hair cascades over the top of her apron—bubbly, gentle, just like her. The sound cuts off abruptly when she notices me. Her body tenses, her eyes narrowing.

"We need to talk," I say quietly.

She glances around the busy cafe and nods towards the back area, currently closed to customers, and nods for me to take a seat at a booth. As I follow her back there, a cold weight settles in my gut. Her world is so bright, so warm—and I'm about to taint it with the darkness of mine. But if I don't, her world could be snuffed out in an instant.

One of her employees wordlessly brings each of us a mug of steaming black coffee and discreetly slips away.

She crosses her arms defensively. "What do you want?"

I take a breath. No turning back now. "I know you want nothing to do with the mafia. But your family's past has put you in danger. There are...interested parties."

Her face pales. I continue, "I can offer you protection, make it clear you're off limits."

She looks away, conflicted. My world terrifies her, but she knows the threat is real.

"Why has this only come about now?"

"Things are happening in the city which are causing debts to be... unforgotten, you might say..."

"This isn't a ploy to get me to turn over my cafe to you for a few weeks like you requested?"

I run my fingers through my hair. "No, Alessia. It's not. I really wish it were that simple."

She frowns, and I can almost see the cogs turning in her head as she processes things. Eventually, she lifts her gaze to meet mine. "And how do I avoid being caught up in this?"

"It would mean a marriage in name only. You remain free to live your life." I keep my voice gentle. This is her choice.

"Marriage?!" Her voice cracks and her gaze flits over me. "To you?"

I nod. "Yes. To me."

Silence stretches between us. Finally she meets my eyes again, fear and resignation swirling in hers. "And if I don't?"

"Your life, your grandmother's life... even your customer's lives," I say, nodding toward the cafe's main area, "could be at risk."

Her eyes grow wide. "You're not just saying this?"

"Know one thing about me, Alessia. I am no joker. And the men who have your name as a target do not play games."

Her gaze meets mine, and I can almost feel her subliminally assessing my words, taking them all in. Finally, she speaks. "Tell me what I need to do."

I let out a breath I didn't realize I was holding. This is the only way to keep her safe.

"It will just be for show," I reiterate. "We continue our lives–separately. But in the eyes of the mafia, you'll be untouchable as my wife."

She flinches at the word 'wife' but nods. "What will this...entail, exactly?" she asks hesitantly. "Living together, pretending to be ma rried..."

"You'll stay in my home for appearances," I say matter-of-factly. "But you'll have your own room, your own privacy. I won't encroach on your life any more than necessary."

I think I see a flash of relief cross her face. She probably expected far worse from a mafia boss.

"And in public, minimal displays of affection should be enough to sell it," I continue. "Nothing that would make you uncomfortable."

She nods slowly, considering. I can see the wheels turning in her mind as she processes it all. This shy cafe manager is handling the upheaval of her life with quiet resilience.

"What about...intimacy?" she asks hesitantly.

I shake my head. "None required. I'll continue my business, you run your cafe. We maintain appearances at formal events, but otherwise, nothing changes."

I can see her turning this over in her mind, her arms wrapped around herself protectively. She's managed to keep separate from this world for so long, but now it's at her doorstep. Sometimes life has a way of showing us who we really are, no matter how much we try to deny it.

"I know it's a lot to take in," I add, softening my tone a fraction. "And it's not ideal. But I give you my word that I only want to help you. And I really think this is the only way to keep you, and your cafe... and your Nonna... safe."

She meets my gaze then, as if judging my sincerity. I hold it unflinchingly. Finally, she sighs.

Alessia takes a deep breath, steadying herself before responding. "I believe you," she says. "I just need...time. To think this over. Talk it through with someone I trust." She glances up at me hesitantly. "Can I have some time?"

I study her for a moment, taking in the tension in her shoulders and the apprehension in her eyes. As much as I want to seal this arrangement immediately, I know she needs space to process everything. After a moment, I nod in understanding. This whole situation has been sprung on her so suddenly. Of course she needs time to wrap her head around the drastic changes to her life.

"Take a couple days," I say finally. "But no more than that. The clock's ticking here."

She nods, relief at my patience flashing across her face. "Thank you. I'll give you my answer soon." I feel an unfamiliar pang in my chest—a desire to put her at ease, which is so unlike me. I'm used to inspiring fear, not comfort.

"Thank you," she murmurs.

We leave it at that for the moment. I can tell the wheels are still turning in her mind, weighing her limited options. She's backed into a corner, but I'll try to make this transition as smooth as possible.

We both stand, the vinyl booth creaking as we slide out. Out of habit, I go to drop a few bills on the table for the untouched coffee, but she waves my hand away and I return them to my wallet.

"Be careful," I tell her seriously. "Don't go anywhere alone. And watch your back."

"I will," she promises.

I turn to leave but pause, looking back at her hovering uncertainly beside the table. "For what it's worth, I'm sorry you got dragged into this. You seem... different from the rest of them."

Something that might be a smile flickers across her lips. "Not sure who 'them' is, or if that's a compliment coming from you."

I huff a quiet laugh. "Take it however you want."

With that, I walk out of the cafe and into the night. As I leave the cafe, I feel the weight of what I've taken on. Sheltering an innocent in the viper's nest of the mafia won't be easy. But the thought of her coming to harm is unacceptable. I push down the voice warning me that this could end badly.

The cold air is bracing after the cozy warmth inside. Hands in my pockets, I make my way down the quiet street, feeling the weight of her decision resting heavily on me. I can only hope I've done enough to convince her. For both our sakes.

For now, all I can do is wait for her decision and prepare for the changes to come in both her life and mine. My gut tells me this arrangement will not leave either of us untouched.

A few days later, she texts me.

Alessia: I'm ready to speak.

I immediately text her back and let her know I'm on my way, and call my driver to pull the car around.

When I arrive at the cafe, she leads me to the same booth where I made the original proposal. For a moment, we sit there in silence. I don't want to pressure her to give me an answer, even though I'm anxious to hear what she has to say.

"Okay," she finally says, so softly I almost don't hear it. Her eyes meet mine, resignation mingling with a tiny spark of defiance. She'll get through this on her own terms.

I admire that fire in her. My world will and has extinguished many, but I suspect her light will endure.

"We have a deal then." I extend my hand.

After a moment, she shakes it, cementing our false union.

A sacrifice of independence to maintain her freedom. The bargain may leave a bitter taste, but it's necessary. Her agreement was only the first part. Mere words. Now we'll see if this fragile arrangement can withstand the dangers yet to come.

I nod, letting go of her hand. Marrying Alessia is merely a practical solution to keep her and her business safe out of some sense of inexplicable obligation, and yet it feels weighted, momentous.

Alessia turns away, her arms wrapped around her curvy frame. She gazes out the nearby window, watching people pass by in the sunlit street. Blissfully unaware of the shadows looming over her.

Over us both now.

I know this charade is the only way to protect her, but doubts gnaw at me. She doesn't belong in my world. Kindness like hers is a liability among the mafia's cold brutality. But then again, she does have deep mafia roots, even though she only learned about them very recently.

Can I really keep her safe? Or am I simply painting a target on her back?

I stare down at the dark liquid swirling in my cup, trying to ignore the weight pressing down on my shoulders. This isn't how I want things to go. Alessia deserves so much more than being dragged into the mire of the mafia underworld. Especially by a man like me, with blood staining his hands. But regardless of my involvement, by sheer chance she seems to be on the precipice of being dragged in anyway. Maybe it's her destiny, with or without me.

"Marco?"

Her soft voice draws me out of my thoughts. I meet her gaze, those warm brown eyes searching my face.

"It's not your fault, you know. You didn't create this...situation."

I huff out a humorless laugh. "Does it matter whose fault it is? You're still stuck with me now."

She tilts her head, a crease forming between her brows. "Why are you doing this? Helping me, I mean."

I look away, staring into my coffee again. How can I begin to explain the tangled mess of duty, guilt, and maybe even a shred of decency that drove me here?

"Let's just say I owe your family a debt from back in the day. Consider us square after this."

"A debt?" she presses. "What kind of debt?"

My jaw tightens, old memories threatening to surface. "It was a long time ago. Back when your father and I were..."

Young. Foolish. Still clinging to our ideals. Before this life hardened us both.

I shake my head sharply. "It doesn't matter now. Point is, I have a responsibility to keep you safe. Whatever it takes."

She falls silent, digesting my words. In the background, the clink of dishes and murmur of patrons carry on, oblivious to the dark bargain being struck.

Finally, Alessia speaks again, her voice soft but steady. "Okay, Marco. I'll trust you on this."

Hearing my name come out of her mouth does things to me. My cock twitches. But now's not the time. I meet her gaze, seeing the fear lingering there but also the quiet determination. She'll face whatever comes with her head held high.

I give a single nod, hoping I can be worthy of her trust.

"Okay then," she nods back. "What happens now?."

I try to keep my expression neutral despite the gravity of what we're discussing.

"I'll make the arrangements. We can finalize the details once you've had some time."

She bites her lip, looking down. I can tell she still isn't fully convinced this is the right path. Not that I can blame her.

Alessia takes a deep breath before facing me again, a forced smile on her lips. "Well, I guess we're engaged then... congratulations?"

Her voice holds a tremor she can't quite disguise. My gut twists, hating that I'm the one to put that fear in her eyes.

"It's just pretend," I say gruffly. "Don't worry, I'll make sure you stay out of the line of fire. It's much easier for me to do that if you're my wife."

She nods, blinking hard. "I know. Thank you, Marco." The words are stilted, like she has to force them out. "I appreciate you...trying to help."

I sigh, shoving my hands in my pockets. "I wish it hadn't come to this. You deserve better."

She gives a sad little laugh. "We play the hand we're dealt. I'll be okay."

Looking at her then, I desperately want to believe that's true. It has to be true.

Six

Alessia

The black sedan glides to a stop outside an imposing iron gate flanked by stone columns. I crane my neck to take in the sheer size of the mansion looming beyond the gate. Intricate metalwork and surveillance cameras line the high perimeter walls. I was expecting his residence to be enormous given the notoriety of his family name, but this is no home—it's a fortress.

While I thought he might accompany me here on my first trip to his home, Marco had a meeting so he sent me on by myself. I'm strangely disappointed not to be spending more time with him, but also relieved that I get to explore his place without his prying eyes. That said, I'm under no illusion that his staff won't just report back anything I say or do. I get the impression that men like him feel like they need to know everything.

The gate swings open and we drive up the long, tree-lined driveway. My palms sweat against the leather seats. What have I gotten myself into?

The car pulls up to the grand portico entrance. I step out on shaky legs into the vast courtyard lined with precisely trimmed hedges and marble statues. Uniformed staff hurry to and fro, averting their gaze. Wow, his team is even bigger than I expected it to be... there must be at least three kinds of uniforms. Garden and maintenance technicians in their dark blue polos, housekeepers in their crisp black and white shirts and aprons, and several others that I can't yet identify.

A stern-looking woman in a crisp suit greets me. "Miss Moretti. This way please." Her heels click sharply as she leads me inside. I guess seeing Marco was busy he sent someone else as a replacement welcoming committee. I'd kind of held out hope that he'd be waiting for me when I got here. Someone who is apparently all business with the bedside manner of a well-fed cat. Maybe he really wasn't lying when he said our marriage would all be just for show. I feel a mixture of relief and, for some unknown reason, slight irritation.

My footsteps echo in the cavernous foyer, marble floors gleaming. A crystal chandelier drips from the domed ceiling. Everything screams old money and power. This is most definitely Marco's world and not mine.

The woman gestures brusquely down a hallway. "Your room is the third door on the left. Dinner is at seven. The security system is active, so do not attempt to leave the premises or the security team will be notified immediately." Her words chill me. They remind me that I'm not a guest here. I'm a prisoner.

I nod mutely and make my way down the hall, each footstep magnified in the hushed atmosphere. My 'room' is larger than my entire apartment, decorated in rich mahoganies and velvets. The canopy bed could sleep four. I find myself blushing as I realize Marco and I could both roll around in the bed with plenty of room left over. I sink into a plush chair by the window overlooking manicured gardens. Somewhere beyond those walls is the city I know, the life I left just this morning, though it feels years away.

A knock at the door startles me. A tall man in a tailored suit enters. He's handsome with a perpetually serious expression and piercing brown eyes. "Miss Moretti, I'm Luca, Mr. De Luca's head of security. I've been asked to give you a tour of the residence."

As we walk, Luca points out the gym, home theater, wine cellar. Security cameras track our every move. The place feels sterile, more like a museum than a home.

We pass a set of double doors. Muffled angry voices leak out. Luca quickens his pace. "Mr. De Luca's study. Private area." His tone brooks no argument.

Marco remains a mystery, glimpsed only in moments like this and the times he's visited the cafe. Powerful, dangerous, unknowable. And I'm at his mercy. In his house. About to be his wife. Just what have I gotten myself into? I barely know him, after all, and here I am in his palatial mansion, about to be made his wife on paper. What if this whole thing is all made up? What if there are no threats beyond the usual that exist living in a big city? What if he's some controlling psychopath who wants to keep me trapped in his basement?

I sigh. If he wasn't so devastatingly handsome, maybe I wouldn't be here. Perhaps I would have turned down his suggestion, laughed it off. But here I am. Am I really that fickle, so easily sucked in by a man? Still, maybe there is truth in his warnings. Maybe I really am a target, and this is the only way to protect my grandmother, my employees and my café.

I continue staring out the window as dusk settles over the grounds below. Somewhere down there, people are wrapping up their normal days, heading home to families, getting ready for a regular evening. While I'm sequestered in this grandiose fortress, my fate in the hands of a virtual stranger who couldn't even make himself available to greet me when I arrived.

What little I know about Marco De Luca only deepens the pit in my stomach. The staff's deference and fear as they avoid his wing of the house. The state-of-the-art security meant to keep threats out...and me in. The heated voices behind closed doors hinting at dealings far beyond the boundaries of my 'normal' world.

I think back to this morning at the cafe when I was steaming milk, joking with customers, blissfully unaware my world was about to be turned upside down. Was it really just a day ago that my life made sense? Now everything is uncertain.

A glance at my phone reminds me there's an outside world, even if I'm cut off from it. At least they didn't take that away from me, although with this level of security I wouldn't be surprised if they insist on that next. I scroll through unanswered texts from friends, photos of places I used to go. Was it naïve to think I could keep one foot in my old reality? Or am I clinging to a life that no longer exists?

My rumbling stomach interrupts my brooding. I debate venturing to the ornate dining room before deciding to make a sandwich in the glossy kitchen instead. Better to keep a low profile, retain small rituals of normalcy.

Looking in his fridge, it's as immaculate as everything else appears to be in the house. No surprises there. But I am pleased to see little touches that make me feel like I'm at home—a thick balsamic glaze, freshly picked basil—presumably from the expansive garden, plump tomatoes that smell like sunshine and goodness.

As I assemble my humble meal, I think of Marco again. Does he stand here in his designer suits, making a snack? Does he have friends who text him silly memes? It's hard to imagine the cold, imposing man indulging in something so...human. For now, I assume that any tasks perceived as menial are done for him by his team, and his days are nothing but serious.

I take my sandwich back upstairs, the marble floors amplifying my footsteps. I'm insignificant here, my life swallowed up in the vast emptiness of this place, dependent on the whims of a powerful and dangerous stranger. A stranger who couldn't even adjust his schedule to be here when I arrived for the first time... for the person who is about to be his wife.

I don't know what this is going to entail, but it can't be as easy as swanning around the mansion making myself sandwiches. At that rate, I might die of boredom. But I must be more than a prisoner in

a gilded cage. I am still me, still Alessia. And I must survive this....
whatever *this* is.

I finish my sandwich, lost in thought. The sound of voices drifts
up from downstairs—Marco must be home. I creep to the top of the
grand staircase and peer between the banisters.

Marco stands in the foyer below, barking orders at his men. His
presence seems to fill the room, commanding attention. The others
listen intently, nodding, ready to obey his every word. This is not a
home—it's a fortress, the headquarters of a vast empire. I need to
remember that. It may have all the trappings of a welcoming residence, but this explains why there's an austere, icy quality to it. Going
through the motions of day-to-day life for the outside world, when the
real business is conducted in the background.

As Marco dismisses the men, a tall woman steps forward hesitantly.
"Mr. De Luca, your godmother called earlier. She asked that you call
her back as soon as possible." Marco's stony expression softens ever so
slightly. "Thank you, Anna. I'll call her after dinner."

So he has a godmother. I mean, I know that many people do... but when I look at someone like Marco, my first thought isn't about their family. I'm struck by this glimpse of Marco's humanity. There is more to him than the ruthless mob boss. What secrets lie beneath that hard exterior? What shaped him into the man he is today?

I hear footsteps on the stairs and scramble back to my room before Marco can discover me spying. My mind spins with more questions than answers. I don't know this man at all. And yet our fates are now intertwined.

I close the door to my lavish prison cell and lean against it, trying to catch my breath. The opulent furnishings that surround me now only magnify how trapped I feel. Like a feral cat misidentified as a fancy pedigree and taken to a fancy mansion, destined to forever feel out of place while spoiled to death. This is not the life I know. And at the same time, I feel both trapped but also guilty for the more basic life I've left behind. I walk over and sink onto the bed, equal parts fascinated and afraid. What have I gotten myself into? I only wonder if the life I led before will ever be the same when I go back to it. Assuming I make it through this.

The Next Morning

My gaze lands on the state-of-the-art coffee maker on the marble countertop in the corner of the room. Of course he has the top-of-the-line model, something that rivals the industrial equipment in any modern coffee shop. Or did he have this especially installed with me in mind? An idea sparks. I rummage through the walk-in closet until I find a small table and chairs. Dragging them to the sitting area, I create a little coffee nook. It's a small act of familiarity amidst the disorientation. A little space to call mine. Let's not even talk about how this room, with its sitting area and walk-in closet, is bigger than my apartment.

As I grind the fragrant beans and watch the dark liquid trickle into the carafe, I feel my nerves settle. The rich aroma transports me back to my cozy café, where I'd chat with regulars while steaming milk for lattes. A world away from this. There, I was able to immerse myself in their hopes, their challenges. Here, I am alone. In a fake relationship with a man I don't even know. A scary man, at that.

I carry my mug to the window and look out at the waking city below. Somewhere down there, my café is opening for the day without me. I wonder if anyone has noticed my absence yet. Do they know where I am or who I'm with? I'm sure my grandmother will adjust the roster and keep things on track, and make up some excuse about why I'm not there. That is, until the truth is revealed. That I'm the next Mrs. Marco De Luca.

I take a sip, letting the taste ground me. No matter how chaotic my life becomes, these quiet moments with coffee remain my sanctuary. The one constant I can count on.

A knock at the door startles me from my thoughts. I take a deep breath and straighten my shoulders, fortifying myself for another day in Marco's world. But inside, a part of me clings to my identity. I am still Alessia Moretti. And I will not be consumed.

I open the door to find Marco's housekeeper, Rosa. She eyes my makeshift coffee corner with pursed lips.

"Mr. De Luca expects you downstairs for breakfast in ten minutes," she says briskly. "He has meetings all morning and wants you ready to accompany him."

I bristle at her tone and the expectation that I'm to just fall in line. "I'll be down when I'm ready. I don't appreciate being summoned like a pet."

Rosa looks shocked. "Miss, the rules of this house are clear. Meals are at set times, and Mr. De Luca expects punctuality."

"Well, he can expect all he wants, but I don't just jump when called," I retort. "I have my own schedule."

Rosa presses her lips together, conflicted. She hurries off, no doubt to report my defiance. I feel a small thrill at challenging the strict order of things, but also an unease at what consequences may follow.

I take my sweet time getting ready, keeping him waiting for at least an additional fifteen minutes. I take a little longer on my makeup and hair, and dawdle while selecting between three perfectly appropriate outfits. As tiny as this flex may be, it feels good to set some type of boundary when things currently feel very one-sided.

At breakfast, the tension between Marco and I is palpable. He watches me with an inscrutable expression as I sip my coffee, refusing to be rushed. Although I can't help but notice the flicker of appreciation as his gaze trails over me. I feel a little warmth in my core under his stare.

"We'll be leaving in five minutes," he states. "I trust you'll be ready."

I meet his gaze. "I'll join you when I'm finished."

His eyes flash, but he simply nods and returns to his newspaper. Another power play.

When we finally leave, Marco opens the car door for me. I pause, surprised by this unexpected courtesy from him. "Thank you," I murmur. As he leans over me to grab the door, I can't help but notice the masculine notes of his aftershave, probably custom-made, and the glow of his freshly shaved, moisturized face with its chiseled jaw. He really is a very handsome man.

He gives me a measured look. "You're welcome."

A subtle shift. We both bend, if only a little.

Later that evening, I'm reading in my room when there's a knock at the door.

"Come in," I call out.

Marco enters, wearing another impeccable suit and looking hot as hell. I can't even begin to imagine the size of his closet, or the roster of seamstresses he must have at his beck and call. My stomach clenches as I realize he's probably fucking them all. "I have some business to attend to. I'll be back late."

I nod, trying not to show my curiosity. Marco rarely explains his comings and goings.

He checks his watch. "I should be going. Rosa's downstairs if you need anything." He pauses. "Help yourself to the kitchen. And the gym, if you'd like. I had some of your favorite songs from the café's playlist loaded into the sound system for you."

I'm surprised by this unprompted hospitality, and a little flustered—both by his attention to detail, and his ability to effortlessly collect personal information on me. Sweet and maybe a little creepy, but I'll take it. "Oh. Thank you."

"You're free to use the amenities here. This is your home too, for now," he says simply.

Again, that subtle shift between us. I'm still wary, but I sense Marco may not be the monster I first thought. At least when he's at home.

After he leaves, I wander the silent halls alone. Despite the luxury, an unease prickles my skin. Marco's world, whatever business he's engaged in, feels dangerous. But it does feel safe being surrounded by his team of security guards and state-of-the-art security equipment. More safe from threats from the outside, at least.

Late at night, I'm startled from sleep by the buzz of my phone. A text from Marco.

Marco: Unforeseen complications. Will be very late. Go back to sleep.

I stare into the darkness, pulse racing. What sinister entanglements keep him out at this hour? For the first time, real fear sinks in about the man I've been bound to. And his texting me makes me feel whatever's keeping him away has something to do with the rival family's interest in me and my family's debt. Otherwise, why would I even be on his mind?

Sleep does not return easily.

Seven

Alessia

The shrill beeping of the alarm clock jars me awake, the glowing red numbers informing me it's 6am. I groan and roll over, burying my face in the plush pillows that engulf me in my massive sleigh bed. The sheets tangled around my legs are made of the softest Egyptian cotton, a luxury I never knew existed back in my modest apartment above the café. I'm normally an early bird, getting up at the crack of dawn to make sure everything is set up for the day, but there's something about this change of pace and the luxurious comfort of my bed that have me craving a sleep-in.

With great effort I peel myself from the cozy nest and make my way to the en-suite bathroom, my bare feet sinking into the plush carpet. I turn the polished chrome knobs in the massive walk-in shower, releasing a cascade of hot water that creates a soothing mist. As I lather the expensive floral shampoo into my hair, I think back to my life just a week ago—showering in a cramped stall, the water sputtering and fluctuating between not quite hot enough and scalding. Not that I ever really dwelled on it, it's just how it was. But so much has changed in such a short time.

After dressing in a casual sundress and pulling my hair into a messy fishtail braid, I make my way downstairs. The marble floors are cold under my feet as I walk past priceless works of art and ornate vases overflowing with fresh flowers. Even after several days here, the opulence still overwhelms me.

In the massive chef's kitchen, the housekeeper, Rosa, greets me warmly. "Buongiorno, signorina! I made your coffee just how you like." I smile gratefully and sip the rich, aromatic brew. It's weird having someone else make coffee for me, but she's done a decent job. And at least this small taste of home still exists in my strange new world.

As I nibble on fresh pastries and yogurt, I hear a gruff voice behind me. "Good morning, Alessia." I turn to see Marco impeccably dressed as always in a crisp suit, his dark eyes regarding me coolly. "I trust you slept well?"

"Yes, thank you," I reply politely. Our exchanges have remained civil, yet distant. He intimidates me with his contained power and brooding presence. His gaze always makes me feel like he's scrutinizing me, assessing my inner thoughts. As if he can see into my mind. I shiver at the thought.

Marco nods curtly and turns to confer with his security team while Rosa refills my coffee. I watch him over the rim of my cup, fascinated by this complex man who has completely upended my life. What secrets lurk behind those unreadable eyes?

I finish my breakfast as Marco and his men discuss business in hushed tones. Their words are lost on me, but the gravity in their voices sends a chill down my spine. This is my life now, whether I want it or not.

As I rise to leave, Marco addresses me. "Alessia, would you join me for a walk in the gardens after breakfast? I'd like to show you the grounds."

I'm surprised by the invitation but nod in agreement. "Of course, that would be nice."

I move to take my plate and cup to the kitchen counter and Rosa waves me away.

We make our way outside, the morning sun warm on our faces. The gardens are straight out of a fairy tale, with sculpted hedges, fountains, and flowers in full bloom. Marco seems to relax ever so slightly as we stroll along the gravel paths.

"My mother loved her roses and hydrangeas," he remarks, gesturing to the rose bushes. "She designed most of these gardens herself."

I'm struck by this personal detail he's chosen to share with me. "They're beautiful," I reply. "Your mother had wonderful taste."

We continue along in silence for a few moments before coming upon a marble bench shaded by a willow tree. Marco gestures for me to sit. I smooth my dress and perch delicately beside him on the cool stone.

"Alessia..." he begins. "I know this situation, our...arrangement, has not been easy for you. And it must feel strange. Especially seeing I've been so busy with work. You must feel like a stranger or a temporary gust here..." He pauses, seeming to choose his words carefully. "But I hope in time you will come to find comfort here. That we may build a certain...understanding between us."

I study his solemn face, allowing his words to settle. "I appreciate that, Marco. You're right... this is all still very new." I take a breath. "But I believe we can find a way to coexist amicably."

He nods, looking thoughtful. For now, an unspoken truce exists between us. What the future holds, only time will tell.

Marco nods slowly, his dark eyes searching my face. "I did not choose this path for us lightly," he says after a moment. "There are ...complications to my life that prevent me from living as other men do."

He looks out over the gardens, a muscle in his jaw twitching. I realize this is likely the most honest he's been with me since I arrived.

"I know you find my world unfamiliar, even frightening at times," he continues. "But believe me when I say I wish only to provide you comfort and safety, as best I can. That's the reason we're doing this, after all. To keep you and those you care about safe from harm."

His voice holds a surprising earnestness. This brief glimpse beneath his stoic facade reveals a depth of character I had not expected.

"I believe you, Marco," I reply gently. "This situation is difficult for us both. But I'm willing to make the best of it, if you are."

The corner of his mouth quirks up slightly. "You continue to surprise me, Alessia. Your compassion does you credit."

I can't help but smile a little in return. Perhaps there is hope for us yet.

Marco gestures to the sprawling gardens surrounding us. "Come, walk with me."

I fall into step beside him along the gravel pathway, the faint scent of roses and jasmine perfuming the air. Marco's home is like an oasis, shut away from the harsh realities of the outside world. Here there is only beauty, calm, and order.

Yet I sense the isolation as well. The cold perfection of the architecture and landscaping speaks of control and restraint. There is little warmth or intimacy. Everything is curated to the finest detail, focused on function over comfort. Impersonal, almost as if you could plug and play any mafia boss into the scenery and they'd blend right in.

Marco walks with an air of contained power, his expression unreadable. The weight of leadership shows in the set of his shoulders, the deliberate pace of his stride. This is a man unaccustomed to idleness or vulnerability.

"Your gardens really are lovely," I offer, hoping to draw him into conversation. They're the one departure I've seen so far from the uniformity of everything else at the residence.

He nods. "I find solace in nurturing living things. Creating order from chaos."

I wonder if he speaks only of the gardens, or of his role as head of the family. As cheesy as it sounds, perhaps being a mafia boss is its own kind of gardening—pruning away unruly shoots, cultivating only what is useful.

We walk in silence for a time. When Marco speaks again, his voice is quiet. "This life of mine can be...solitary. I bear responsibilities few can understand."

He turns to gaze at me and pauses, weighing his words. "Having you here provides a rare moment of respite. Your presence is...not unwelcome."

I'm surprised by this admission, despite its formal delivery. Have I become more to him than just a business transaction? He barely knows me. The thought leaves me conflicted, but also intrigued to know this complicated man better.

Where this startling new connection between us might lead, I can't yet say. But the seeds of understanding have been planted. I'm touched by Marco's unexpected candor. Beneath the hard exterior, there are layers I'm only beginning to uncover.

We continue walking, the afternoon sun warm on our faces. Marco seems lost in thought, his gaze introspective.

"What drew you to the café business?" he asks.

I tell him about my family's history, my Nonna's recipes, the joy of making food with love. Of building community, one perfect cappuccino at a time.

Marco listens intently, asking thoughtful questions. He confides he often longs for the simple pleasures—a quiet meal with friends, the comfort of familiar places.

"Perhaps you could show me your Nonna's recipes sometime," he suggests tentatively.

My eyes widen in surprise. I imagine this powerful man in my tiny café kitchen, sleeves rolled up, kneading dough. Marco wants to experience my world. Of course, if I'm going to teach him to cook my family's recipes it's going to be in his state-of-the-art kitchen that would leave most professional chefs drooling. But I think I can cope with that.

We talk and laugh over a late lunch. The conversation flows easily now. Marco's smile reaches his eyes, lighting his face with warmth.

I nod appreciatively as Marco shares more of himself—small details that hint at the man behind the mask. He describes summers in Tuscany as a boy, running through sun-dappled olive groves. The scent of fresh baked foccaccia with olives from the village bakery. How he still seeks out that bread to remind him of simpler times.

In turn, I tell him about my parents, their boundless love and support. How they worked tirelessly to give me opportunities they never had.

"Family is everything," Marco says quietly. Though his parents are gone, I sense their influence still guides him. Just like mine guide me.

Later, Marco joins me in the music room. Marco settles comfortably in an armchair, his expression relaxed and engaged. Before really thinking about it, I sit at the grand piano and play a melancholy sonata. Closing my eyes, I lose myself in the ebb and flow of notes. It's been years since I played, but they say playing the piano is a bit like getting back on a bike after many years, and the notes flow to me effortlessly.

When I finish, Marco's expression is raw, vulnerable. "My mother used to play that piece," he says thickly. "You brought her back to me."

He turns away, overcome by emotion. My heart aches for his profound loss. One that I understand far too deeply. Slowly, I come to stand beside him. It feels comfortable being next to him, a far cry from the first time he visited the cate.

With time, I hope Marco will share more happy memories of his parents. For now, a chord of understanding begins to resonate between us. Walls are falling away, revealing two surprisingly kindred spirits despite our significantly different upbringings. I can see that, despite the rumors that swirl around his family name, inside of this handsomely curated exterior is a human being with childhood memories and traumas that impact him every day.

Despite the growing connection between us, an undercurrent of tension remains ever-present. This forced union strains against our true desires. I still ache for my simple life at the café, even though now that seems like a distant dream. I'm scared that if I ever do go back, I could put my employees and my customers at risk... my Nonna. Maybe they already are in danger, even while I'm cocooned safely here. That doesn't seem fair. Maybe I've made a mistake.

Marco's world frightens me. Behind the decadent trappings lie unseen dangers. I know so little of his business, shrouded in secrecy. Only glimpses of his ruthless power filter through. I worry that his ruthlessness could turn on me at any moment.

Like the other night, when Marco took an urgent call that sent him storming into the night. I peered through the curtains watching him speed off, tires screeching. A cold dread filled me, wondering what darkness he raced towards.

Even in the sanctuary of this house, I can't escape the looming threat. Marco's men are never far away, constantly vigilant. I'm reminded this gilded cage still locks me in. I know I'm being watched, the many cameras sprinkled around the home and grounds a constant reminder that I can't fully let my guard down.

Marco sensing my unease, makes efforts to reassure me. But I know he shields me from the truth. At any moment, violence could erupt and shatter our fragile peace.

So I cling to these quiet moments we share, suspended in time. Aware they may be fleeting. Marco too seems to savor our talks, as one savors the last golden days before winter. An unspoken question hangs between us—how long can this last? What will the point be when things come to an end and go back to normal, or otherwise.

For now, we carry on, neither of us ready to voice our true feelings. But the deeper we connect, the harder it becomes to ignore the gathering storm.

The next evening, I'm reading in the library when Marco enters, his shirt splattered with blood. I gasp, my book tumbling to the floor.

"Are—are you okay?" I ask, panicked.

"It's not mine," he says gruffly.

My pulse races as I take in his disheveled appearance. His knuckles are bruised, his face etched with a cold fury I've never seen before.

"What happened?" I ask shakily.

He pours himself a scotch from the decanter on the bar cart that sits against one of the library walls, downing it in one gulp.

"Just business. Nothing for you to worry about."

We haven't known each other long, but I know better than to press him. Instead, I cautiously approach and begin cleaning the blood from his hands with a warm cloth. He tenses at first but soon relaxes under my gentle touch.

We don't speak. The only sound is the crackling fireplace. I feel his eyes on me as I carefully wipe the last of the stains away, revealing grazed and swollen knuckles beneath.

"You shouldn't see such things," he says finally, his voice uncharacteristically soft.

I meet his gaze. "I knew what I was getting into. I'm still here."

Something flickers in his stormy eyes. Before I can decipher it, he turns abruptly and stalks out.

Alone again, I shiver despite the heat of the fire. I know Marco was reminding me, in his own way, of the violence that surrounds him. That I shouldn't get too comfortable in this temporary oasis.

But as darkness falls, I make my decision. I will not run or hide from whatever comes.

Marco's world may be perilous, but it is one I now share.

For better or worse.

Eight

Marco

The thunder rumbles outside like a caged beast, rattling the window panes of my quiet library. I sit alone, nursing a glass of scotch as I watch the storm brewing over the bay. The tumultuous skies match the turmoil in my heart.

Usually my home hums with activity—my men coming and going, deliveries being made, business being conducted. But tonight, an eerie silence pervades. I've given orders to be left alone, to have time to think.

My mind turns to my father, who sat in this same leather chair, staring out at the same angry seas when he was conflicted about family, loyalty, and love. I feel the weight of his legacy pressing down on me now in the gloom. The choices I make seal fates and end lives, for better or worse.

This life isolates me from the world outside these walls. I'm set apart, elevated and feared. No one truly knows me or sees the doubts

I harbor deep within. I take another burning sip, wondering if the emptiness will ever subside...

I nod to Alessia as she enters the room, the click of her heels muted by the plush rug. She's shed the trendy sundresses and updos, wearing a simple sweater and jeans, her hair loose around her shoulders. It makes her seem younger, more approachable. Although whatever she wears, I know one thing to be true—she's the most stunning woman I've ever laid eyes on.

She glances at the tumbler in my hand. "Rough day?"

I let out a wry laugh. "You could say that."

She settles on the leather couch across from me, tucking her feet underneath her in a way that makes me want to rush over there and envelop her in my arms. But of course, I don't. I stay fixed in my chair, trying to figure out what comes next.

"You know," she says, "I always pictured mafia bosses presiding over raucous parties and gambling dens, not sitting alone in dark rooms."

"The dark rooms come after the parties," I reply ruefully.

She smiles a little at that, her eyes scanning the bookshelves.

"Have you read all of these?"

I nod. "Most of them. This room was my sanctuary growing up."

She pulls out a worn copy of The Great Gatsby, flipping through the pages.

"This was always one of my favorites. It made me want to move to another city and reinvent myself."

Her voice grows wistful. I study her face, recalling my own youthful dreams before the weight of my name came crashing down...

The rain patters against the glass, cocooning us in this private moment. I realize I barely know this woman who fate has entwined me with. But for the first time, I realize I want to do more than just protect her.

I take a slow sip of whiskey, gathering my thoughts. It's rare I share these pieces of myself. But something in her open expression compels me.

"When I was seven, my father gave me a chess set. He said if I could beat him, he'd take me on my first job with him."

I absently turn the tumbler in my hand. "I spent hours studying those black and white pieces, learning strategies, practicing end games. Chess requires patience, foresight, and total discipline. I had to master it all."

I meet her gaze. "It took a year of relentless work before I finally won. I'll never forget the grin on my father's face when he said 'Checkmate'."

Rain patters against the windowpanes, filling the thoughtful silence.

"What was the job?" she finally asks.

My jaw tightens. "Nothing a seven-year-old should see."

Understanding flickers in her eyes. This life forced me to grow up fast, to harden parts of myself that should've stayed soft.

"I'm sorry you had to go through that." Her voice is gentle, without judgment.

I give a slight shrug, the most vulnerability I can allow right now. But her quiet acceptance soothes something in me.

We sit awhile, two strangers connected by a story. The storm rages on outside, but here, just for now, there is stillness.

I nod slowly, appreciating her compassion. Our arranged union threw us together, but only now are we truly seeing each other.

"What about you?" I ask. "Any childhood dreams before all this?"

She looks thoughtful, a crease forming between her brows. "You know, I guess I really was living my dream. I always imagined having a little café someday. Nothing fancy, just cozy and full of delicious smells—fresh bread, cinnamon, coffee."

Her features soften as she describes it, linking her childhood dreams to her recent past. I can still picture her there, bustling around in an apron, chatting with customers. It suits her. I feel like a monster for dragging her away. But if I had let her stay in her old life, she may not still be here...

"Why a café, though? Did you consider a restaurant or a bar... some other kind of food place?"

"My nonna owned one back in Italy. I'd spend summers there, watching her work. The care she put into everything, how people lingered for hours..." She trails off, lost in the memory. "And then she brought this business when we immigrated. She handed it over to me, but still is heavily involved, and does all the bookkeeping and so on."

"It sounds nice," I offer. And it does. A glimpse of the life she could've continued to have had, before her father's long-ago dealings changed everything.

"Maybe someday." She gives a small shrug, but there's longing in her voice.

We fall into easy silence again. For these stolen moments, we aren't reluctant spouses. Just two people sharing pieces of who we are underneath it all.

The storm still rages outside, but here, we've found a moment of quiet.

Alessia's words hang in the air between us, this talk of simpler dreams that now feel well and truly out of reach. I know that longing all too well.

"I never wanted any of this," I admit quietly.

Her eyes find mine, intent. She doesn't have to ask what I mean.

"As a kid, I just wanted to play football and go fishing with my cousins. Maybe attend a rock concert every now and then." I huff a humorless laugh. "Not exactly Don material."

"So why did you?" she asks gently.

I rub my jaw, buying time. No one's ever asked so plainly before.

"My father chose this path long before I was born. After he was killed, it fell to me to take over the family business." I shrug, as if it were that simple. As if I'd had any real choice.

She studies me for a moment. "Do you ever wonder what might have been?"

The question lands heavily. I try not to dwell on roads not taken, but late at night, I still do.

"Sometimes," I admit. "Mostly, I wonder about the man I might have become."

Without the weight of the mafia on my shoulders, twisting me, hardening me. Without blood on my hands.

Alessia nods slowly, like she understands. Her father's legacy chains her too in its own way.

"It's not too late, you know." Her voice is soft but fierce. "To find that man again."

I want to believe her. That I could still choose who I become, even now. But the darkness runs too deep in me.

Doesn't it?

I'm caught off guard by the intensity in her eyes. Like she can see right through to the core of me.

"I appreciate the thought, but men like me don't get second chances," I say ruefully. "I've made my bed, and the rest of my life feels very mapped out to me."

She tilts her head, a crease forming between her brows. "Why not?"

"Too much blood on my hands." I flex them unconsciously. "Can't outrun the past."

"Maybe not," she says. "But you can still shape the future."

I'm struck by her stubborn faith despite everything she knows about me. The things I've done.

"You have a big heart, Alessia." I give her a small, sad smile. "Don't lose that. Being around men like me can tarnish people like you."

She flushes slightly at the unexpected compliment.

We lapse into a thoughtful silence, both absorbed in our own reflections. The storm rages on outside, but in this room, just for now, there is light.

I don't know what any of this means for us. If this fragile trust can withstand the hurricane force winds waiting just beyond that door.

But in this moment, I feel the first small stirrings of hope.

I take a deep breath, trying to steady the sudden swirl of emotions in my chest. This evening has cracked open something in me, something I've kept locked away for a long time. I'm not sure I'm ready to confront whatever waits on the other side.

Alessia seems to sense my inner turmoil. She reaches over and gently lays her hand on mine. Just that simple touch ignites my skin.

"It's getting late," she says softly. "We should try to get some rest."

I nod, not trusting my voice. As she stands, her fingers trail lightly across my knuckles. Such a small thing, but it shakes me to my core.

She bids me goodnight and I listen to her footsteps fade down the hall. Alone again, I rake my hands through my hair. This woman unravels me in ways I don't fully comprehend.

I've always prided myself on being in control. Of my emotions, my reactions, every aspect of my life. But Alessia makes me feel off-balance, like I'm standing on uncertain ground.

With her, I find myself saying and doing things I never imagined. Revealing secrets I've never shared. Feeling things I swore I never would.

It terrifies me. But it also exhilarates me in a way I've never known.

I stare out at the storm, more confused than ever. The rules have changed, the game redefined. I don't know how to protect my heart when I can't even understand my own feelings.

But as lightning splits the sky, illuminating the darkness, I make a silent vow. I will not let the ghosts of my past dictate my future. Not this time.

For once in my life, I will fight for something real. Something that feels like hope.

Nine

Alessia

I wake to the smell of frying garlic and basil. It's hard to explain, but I immediately know that Marco must be cooking in the kitchen. I stretch beneath the silk sheets, the morning light filtering through the curtains.

My bare feet meet the cold marble floor as I make my way downstairs, tying my robe around my waist. Marco stands at the stove, sleeves rolled up, wrist flicking as he tosses mushrooms in the pan. He looks even more attractive than I imagined, his broad shoulders and forearms rippling each time he flicks the pan.

"Buongiorno," he says without turning.

"Something smells amazing."

"Just a little breakfast."

I pour myself some coffee and sit at the counter. Marco plates two omelets, handing me one.

"Grazie."

We eat in silence. He reads the paper while I gaze out the window at the climbing roses along the garden wall. I never pictured this. Waking up to Marco cooking breakfast, sharing these quiet moments.

"I have a meeting later," he says, breaking the silence. "But I found this in a used bookstore yesterday."

He slides a worn copy of *Haunting Adeline* across the counter. I run my fingers over the embossed cover.

"You remembered it's my favorite."

Marco shrugs, but I catch the hint of a smile.

"Who knew you were such a dark romance lover? A connoisseur of smut?" I say playfully.

He snorts. "Don't get any ideas."

But as we banter over breakfast, I feel something shift between us. A blurring of lines. In these simple moments, we are no longer enemies bound by convenience. Just two souls sharing a meal, enjoying each other's company.

Perhaps we are more than either of us realized.

I smile to myself as I wash the breakfast dishes, the warm water soothing my hands. Marco disappeared into his office after we ate, off to handle "business" no doubt. I don't ask too many questions about his work. Plausible deniability and all that. And I still don't feel like it's my place.

As I'm drying the last plate, a wave of dizziness hits me. I grip the counter to steady myself. Must be coming down with something. I make my way upstairs to lie down, each step an effort.

I collapse into bed, pulling the covers up to my chin. My limbs feel heavy, my head throbbing. My body trembles despite the warmth of the covers, and eventually I drift into a feverish sleep.

Sometime later, I'm startled awake by a cool hand on my forehead. Marco sits at the edge of the bed, brow furrowed.

"You're burning up," he says.

"It's just a cold or something," I rasp. "I'll be fine."

He shakes his head, reaching for the nightstand. "Here, take this."

I swallow the pills and sip the glass of water he holds to my lips. His hand lingers beneath my head, gentle.

"Get some rest. I'll check on you in a bit."

He brushes a strand of hair from my face before getting up to leave. I close my eyes, comforted knowing he's near. Despite my illness making we feel awful, his touch is comforting and even a little exciting.

Over the next few days, Marco cares for me tirelessly between his work obligations. He brings soup, extra blankets, cold compresses for my head. His touch is tender when he helps me sit up or take medicine. No demands or expectations, just a simple desire to nurse me back to health.

In my rare lucid moments, I study his handsome face hovering above me, etched with concern. This man who I thought incapable of real human connection.

As my fever finally breaks, our eyes meet in silent understanding. Something fractured in both of us has begun to heal.

I'm finally feeling well enough to get out of bed and move around the house some. Marco is in his home office, the door partially open.

I pause in the hallway, watching him work with impressive levels of intensity and focus. His shirt sleeves are rolled up, revealing the tattoos snaking up his forearms. God, how I love a man with tattoos. And a powerful man with tattoos is even hotter.

So different from the starched suits and cufflinks he wears to conduct business. In these private moments, his rough edges show through the polished veneer.

I'm drawn from my thoughts as the front door opens and two of Marco's men stride in. They nod curtly in my direction before continuing to the office.

"The shipment's ready to move," one says. Marco's demeanor shifts, his expression hardening as he discusses logistics.

This stark contrast hits me once again. The man who gently cared for me these past days also ruthlessly runs an international crime syndicate. My sickness allowed us to briefly forget the tangled circumstances binding us together. But the real world always encroaches again.

Marco glances up and catches my eye through the open door. Something softens in his gaze for a moment before he turns back to his men.

"Make sure there aren't any loose ends. I don't want trouble with the local families." His voice is steely.

I slip away, my steps heavy. However Marco makes me feel, I cannot ignore the danger surrounding him. My family would likely benefit from this arrangement. They haven't explicitly said they expect me to gain his trust for our own purposes, yet clearly it places us at an advantage. But my heart threatens to betray that mission.

I take a deep breath as I enter the kitchen, busying myself with mundane tasks like brewing coffee and prepping ingredients for dinner. The domesticity of it helps ground me after the intrusion of Marco's business. Plus, it feels good to be doing something after spending days in bed feeling weak and hopeless.

Soon I hear footsteps approaching. Marco's men must have left as he comes into the kitchen alone, his shirt sleeves still rolled up.

"Everything okay, Alessia?" he asks, glancing at me. "You sure you should be up and about already? Take the time you need to rest and recuperate."

"Of course, I'm fine," I reply lightly, not meeting his eyes. Marco comes closer, his voice lowered.

"You know I don't want you involved in any of that." He gestures vaguely in the direction of his office.

I pause my chopping, knife poised over the cutting board. "It's your world, Marco. I can't pretend it doesn't exist."

He runs a hand over his jaw, seeming unsure how to respond. The air feels heavy between us.

Finally Marco moves closer, gently taking the knife from my hand and setting it down. He turns me to face him, his eyes intent on mine.

"This..." he trails off, his hand lightly grazing my cheek. "Us...it's more than just business now."

My pulse quickens at his touch, his words. I know he's right. Our relationship has shifted over these past weeks. But neither of us has dared to speak it aloud until now.

"Marco..." His name comes out almost as a whisper. I hold my breath as he leans in, his piercing eyes fixed on me, and I feel myself drawn like a moth to flame, consequences be damned. Just before our lips meet, a shrill ring cuts through the charged air. Marco pulls back with a muttered curse, reaching into his pocket for his phone. His jaw tightens as he glances at the screen.

"I have to take this."

I nod mutely, my cheeks flaming as I turn back to the cutting board. Marco's tone is clipped and cold as he answers. I try not to eavesdrop, focusing on dicing vegetables with trembling hands.

But I can't ignore the ugly truth invading our fragile moment. Marco's world—the danger, the violence—it's always lurking. No matter how much we pretend otherwise, it won't just disappear because we wish it would.

Marco ends the call and lets out a long breath, scrubbing a hand over his face. When he meets my eyes again, the warmth from before is gone. In its place is a hard glint, the stoic mask of the mafia boss firmly back in place.

"I'm sorry, I have to go out tonight. Business." Marco's voice is detached, all business once more.

I nod, offering a weak smile that doesn't reach my eyes. "Of course. Dinner will be waiting when you're back."

Marco gazes at me for a beat as if he wants to say more. His hand stretches out, almost involuntarily, and brushes against mine. But then he suddenly yanks it back and turns on his heel, the moment shattered beyond repair. The door clicks shut behind him with an air of grim finality.

I stand frozen, emotions churning within me. I thought I could handle this, but the reality is so much messier and more painful than I ever imagined. I don't know how to reconcile my feelings for Marco with the ruthless world he inhabits. But I do know one thing—this can only end in heartbreak. I need to protect myself.

I let out a shaky breath as the echo of Marco's footsteps fades down the hall. The looming silence of this big, empty house closes in on me, emphasizing just how alone I am.

Hugging my arms around myself, I retreat to the living room and sink down onto the couch, emotions crashing over me in waves. I blink back the hot tears that spring unbidden to my eyes. Crying won't change anything. I knew what I was getting into when I agreed to this marriage. Marco never made any promises of a normal life.

But I can't ignore the way my heart clenches every time he walks out that door into danger. I can't pretend it doesn't destroy me to watch him close himself off again and again, hiding behind that impenetrable mask.

I'm terrified of losing him. The thought of never seeing Marco again, of him disappearing into the darkness of his world, it's unbearable. We're not close, but I'm starting to feel feelings. It's hard not to, I'm bound to care about those I'm close to and he's the only person I'm spending any time with, as rare as it is. But what choice do I have? I'm just supposed to sit here helplessly while he risks his life over and over? I don't even know this man, really. Yet each time we have an interaction, I see him... the man behind the mask... and I want to know more of him.

I bury my face in my hands, choking back a sob. When did I let this happen? When did I allow myself to care so deeply for Marco despite all the warnings?

Love isn't rational. It creeps up on you when you least expect it, regardless of all the reasons you shouldn't give in to it. And now my heart is paying the price, beginning to fall for a man who I don't really know and who I can never really have.

Ten

Marco

A chill runs down my spine as I hang up the phone. News of the Di Gregorio family mobilizing their men can only mean one thing—they're making a move against us.

I bark orders, sending more guards to patrol the grounds and posting lookouts on the walls. My mind races through the implications. We've had an uneasy truce with the Di Gregorios for years now, but if they've decided to challenge me, this will not end well for them.

Alessia steps into my office, her brow furrowed with concern. "What's going on, Marco? I saw men rushing about and heard you shouting."

She moves closer until her hand rests on my arm, her warmth seeping through my sleeve. I take a deep breath, the tension in my shoulders easing. Even now, her touch has a calming effect. She doesn't usually ask me questions about my work, which is the way I prefer it, but something about tonight is different.

I pull her close, wrapping my arms around her. "There's trouble brewing with a rival family. It was already getting dangerous with some other groups, but now more information has come to light about a particularly ruthless syndicate. I have to take some precautions."

She tenses in my embrace. "Will there be fighting? Are we in danger?"

"Not if I can help it," I say. "But we have to be prepared."

Alessia looks up at me, her blue eyes normally full of optimism and hope now clouded with worry. My chest tightens. I never wanted her to be embroiled in this world and its endless violence. But now she's mine, tied to me in more ways than one, and I will keep her safe no matter the cost.

"I won't let anything happen to you," I vow, cupping her face in my hands. "You're under my protection now, my love, and no one will get past me to harm you. Do you understand?"

She nods, some of the tension easing from her body. I kiss her then, slow and deep, reaffirming my promise and chasing away the specter of danger that hovers at the edge of our newfound bliss. War may be looming, but in this moment, she is all that matters. I will face any battle to keep her by my side.

She leaves my study and I sleep little, making preparations to defend our turf.

The next morning, I find Alessia in the kitchen talking to Carmela, one of the housekeepers. Their voices are hushed, and they stop speaking altogether when I enter the room.

Alessia smiles, but it doesn't reach her eyes. She's a terrible liar. It's clear my staff have filled her in on the situation, trying to reassure her in their own way.

I nod at Carmela. "Leave us."

She scurries off, casting a sympathetic glance at Alessia and a guilty look in my direction. Gossips, all of them. I'll deal with that later. I pull Alessia into my arms, feeling the tension in her body. "There's no need to worry," I say. "I have everything under control."

"That's not very reassuring...I feel like you're trying to placate me like I'm some ignorant little girl." She looks up at me, brows furrowed.

"Marco, I'm not naive. I know how dangerous your world is. And now I'm a part of it, for better or for worse."

Her words strike a chord in me. She's right—she is in danger simply by being with me. I brought her into this life, ironically to protect her, and now it's my duty to shield her from its harsh realities. But how long can I possibly keep her safe? I thought keeping her close by my side would mark her as off limits to our rivals, but in doing so I may have inadvertently placed a target on her back.

"Besides," she adds, placing her hand on my shoulder and gazing deep into my eyes, "wasn't that the point of all this? I would have been in even more danger had you not rode into my café on your imaginary white horse to save me by bringing me to this castle of yours?"

I smirk and then tighten my hold on her, as if I can protect her through sheer force of will. But in my gut, I know a storm is coming. And when it hits, it will descend upon us with a vengeance.

Alessia

The tension in the house is palpable for days. Marco barely sleeps, constantly on alert and barking orders at his men. I try to avoid his brooding silences, sensing his preoccupation.

One morning, I venture into the gardens for some fresh air. The bodyguards stationed around the perimeter make me uneasy, a reminder of the threat looming over us.

A sharp crack in the bushes has me whirling around. But it's only a stray cat prowling around. I breathe a sigh of relief, feeling foolish.

Another snap behind me. I freeze in my tracks, heart pounding. Slowly, I turn to find a man emerging from the foliage, gun pointed directly at me.

"Well, hello there, sweetheart," he says with a twisted grin. "Aren't you a pretty little thing?"

I gasp, stumbling back. The man continues advancing, eyes glinting with menace. "The boss man's new plaything, hmm? This should be fun. Alessia, I believe?" He ogles me, his eyes trailing over my body.

I shiver under the weight of his gaze, the sound of my name on his lips, and the gun he points directly at me as he advances on me.

He reaches out to grab my arm, and I scream. Shots ring out before I can draw breath, and the man collapses with a cry.

Marco storms into view, chest heaving with rage as he fires again at the lifeless body. He kicks the gun away, then pulls me into his arms. I cling to him, shaking uncontrollably.

Marco's hands roam over me, checking for injuries with frantic urgency. "Are you hurt? Did he touch you?" His eyes blaze, and I know if the man were still alive, Marco would tear him limb from limb.

"I'm fine," I gasp out. "Just scared."

Marco crushes me against him, one hand on the back of my head. "I'm sorry, tesoro," he says, voice rough with emotion. "I never should have let my guard down."

Over his shoulder, I glimpse the dead man's face, now frozen in a mask of terror. Bile rises in my throat at the sight, a gruesome reminder of the world I now inhabit. A world where a quiet morning in the garden can descend into violence at any moment. I'd like to say it's the first dead body I've ever seen in real life, but living in the city makes that something you unfortunately can't avoid. That said, I've never seen the body of someone who's tried to kill me...or kissed the person who killed them in cold blood. That's a new one.

Marco is right—he can never let his guard down. And as long as I'm by his side, apparently neither can I. I shiver at the thought of what might have happened if Marco hadn't proposed this arrangement. I would have been alone at the café, which is obviously a mob target, owing a mafia debt I knew nothing about. Endangering everybody I ever cared about because of a family legacy I never knew I was part of.

Marco pulls back to study my face, brow furrowed in concern. "Are you sure you're alright?"

I swallow and nod. "Yes. I'm fine now."

His gaze darkens. "I won't let anyone hurt you. Do you understand? Anyone who threatens you will suffer the consequences."

A shiver runs down my spine at the implacable tone in his voice. I know he means every word—for my sake, Marco would unleash hell on earth.

"I know," I whisper.

Marco's expression softens. "Good. Now, let's get you inside."

He steers me toward the house, one arm wrapped securely around my waist. I lean into him, drawing strength from his solid presence.

The chaos of the shootout still echoes in my mind, replaying on a loop like a macabre film reel. I squeeze my eyes shut, trying to block out the images, but it's no use. Each step brings a new wave of trembling, and by the time we reach the front door, I'm shaking apart.

Marco scoops me into his arms without a word and carries me upstairs to my room. Placing me gently on my the ground, he walks me backwards until my back hits the wall, pressing his body flush against mine. I can feel his arousal through the layers of clothing, hard and insistent against my hip.

He leads me over to my bed where he sits on the edge, settling me in his lap and wrapping his arms around me. I cling to him, craving the warmth and steadiness of his body. He holds me close, stroking my hair and murmuring soft words of comfort.

Gradually, the trembling subsides, leaving behind a bone-deep exhaustion. I sag against Marco with a sigh, suddenly feeling wrung out and hollow.

"There now, it's alright," he soothes. "You're safe."

Safe. The word elicits a pang of sorrow and bitterness. Nowhere is truly safe, not in this world we inhabit. Danger lurks around every corner, violence always waiting to erupt at a moment's notice.

Marco kisses the top of my head, his embrace tightening. "Don't be afraid, Alessia," he says, as if reading my thoughts. "I told you I would keep you safe, and I always keep my promises."

His vow should reassure me, but instead, it only brings a renewed wave of fear. Because Marco can't control the demons that stalk us, any more than I can escape the life I now lead. And as long as we're together, there will always be a target on our backs.

I lift my head to meet Marco's gaze, seeing my own troubled thoughts reflected in his eyes. "What are we doing?" I whisper. "How can this ever work?"

"I don't know," he admits. "But I do know that I can't give you up. Not now, not ever."

His words make my heart clench. I know with sudden, blinding clarity that I can't give Marco up either. That against all odds and reason, I have fallen deeply, irrevocably in love with this complicated, dangerous man.

"Marco," I breathe, cupping his cheek. He leans into my touch, eyes closing for a brief moment. "The truth is, you're not the only one who can't walk away."

His eyes fly open, staring at me with a mix of hope and disbelief. "What are you saying?"

"I'm saying that I think I'm falling in love with you," I tell him. "Despite everything, you've become the best part of my life. And if being with you means living with fear and uncertainty, then so be it. I'll face any danger for the chance to be by your side."

Marco's breath leaves him in a rush. For a long moment he simply gazes at me, emotions flickering across his face too quickly to read. Then he surges forward, claiming my lips in a searing kiss.

It's a kiss filled with passion and possession, marking me as surely as any brand. When we finally break apart, Marco presses his forehead to mine, his ragged breaths mingling with my own.

"You're sure about this?" His voice is rough with some indefinable emotion. "If you bind yourself to me, there's no going back. The life I lead...it won't be an easy one. There will be times I have to put my duties first, no matter the cost."

"I know," I say. "Just as there will be times when I have to accept the woman I once was in order to survive. We can't change who we are, Marco. But if we face each new challenge together, I believe we can build a future. Our future."

Marco smiles then, slow and breathtaking. "Our future," he echoes, sealing his promise with another searing kiss.

My hands tangle in Marco's hair as the kiss deepens, desire pooling low in my belly.

A soft moan escapes me when Marco's lips trail down my neck, nipping and sucking at my sensitive skin. His hands roam over my body, skimming up my sides before cupping my breasts. I arch into his touch with a gasp.

"Tell me to stop," Marco rasps, "and I will. I don't want to push you into something you're not ready for."

"Don't you dare stop," I say breathlessly.

Marco growls in approval, swiftly unbuttoning my blouse. My bra soon follows, baring my breasts to his heated gaze. He lowers his head, taking one rosy nipple into his mouth, sucking gently at first before teasing it with his tongue and teeth. I cry out, my fingers digging into his shoulders.

"That's it," he whispers against my skin. "Let go, baby."

Somehow, I manage to unclasp his necklace and throw it aside as he continues to worship my breasts. My heart races as his hands slide up my thighs, pushing my skirt up inch-by-inch till it pools at my waist. He kneels before me, kissing and nibbling his way up my leg.

He gazes up at me intensely from the apex of my thighs and the sight of him just about makes me lose my mind.

"Marco," I whimper, my head falling back against the pillow. His name is a plea and a prayer.

"Tell me what you want, Alessia," he breathes, spreading me open with his fingers. "Tell me what feels good."

"Everything," I groan. "You."

He chuckles darkly, his hot breath fanning over my wetness. And then his tongue dives inside me, causing me to gasp and grab a fistful of his hair. His tongue flicks against my clit, sending shockwaves of pleasure through my core. It's been so long since I've felt anything like this—raw, intense longing. I cry out as he buries his face between my legs, pressing his mouth to my pussy. I'm lost in the sensation of his lips and teeth, the scrape of his stubble against my sensitive skin.

His tongue circles my clit, driving me wild with each lick and suck.

"I'm close," I whisper, my voice hoarse. "Marco... I'm close."

And then he sucks hard on my clit, and I explode beneath him. I cry out his name as he continues to thrust, sending us both over the edge. My walls clench around him, and he growls before pouring his seed deep inside me. We collapse onto the bed, our hearts pounding in unison.

"That's it, baby," he mumbles against me. "Give it to me." I can imagine his erection pressing against me, and I want it inside me so badly.

He moves back up my body and kisses me deeply. I respond, our need for each other tangible. I slide my hand down his chest and grab his cock, guiding it towards my entrance. He hesitates for a moment before pushing inside, filling me slowly but surely. We both gasp as he slowly thrusts in and out, our hips meeting with a rhythm. It's messy, urgent, and so damn right. His moans echo against my lips, mixing with my own gasps for air. His hands grip my hips tightly, pulling me closer into each stroke, and I can feel the anger and lust intertwined in every movement.

"More," I murmur, arching my back. He obliges, plowing into me rougher, faster, sending sparks of pleasure through my whole body. My nails dig into his shoulders, leaving half-moons in the flesh.

"Fuck, Alessia," he growls. "You're so tight." The bed creaks under our combined weight as we move together, our bodies slapping together in a primal dance.

The aftermath is a blur to me, as intimate as the moment has been. Marco rolls off me, his heavy breathing synced with mine. I feel the sweat cooling between us, and I can't help but trace his jawline with my fingertips. The stubble scratches my skin lightly.

"Stay here," he says, his voice rough. He gets up, leaving the room momentarily, returning with a warm, damp washcloth. He cleans me up gently, his touch a stark contrast to the rough sex we just had.

As I watch him, I can't help but think about the irony of our situation. Just hours ago, he felt like a stranger who I was just beginning to know. Now we're tangled in sweaty sheets, our bodies intertwined like two humans who've just valiantly fought for survival. It doesn't quite seem real.

We're silent for a while, lying there in each other's arms. Eventually, Marco speaks up. "You know this changes nothing, right?" he says, his voice low.

I nod against his chest. "I know." But I don't really. Because suddenly, everything feels different.

Outside, the sounds of chaos continue—sirens wailing in the distance, people shouting orders, guns cocking. It's a stark reminder of the reality we live in. A part of me wishes we could stay here forever, safe in our little bubble... but I know it's not possible.

Marco pulls back to look at me, studying my face. "Was it good for you?" He asks, his voice a raspy whisper.

I nod, unable to meet his gaze. My heart thunders in my ears, and I feel a blush creep up my neck. It's not just because of the physical pleasure—it's because this man, this ruthless criminal, just made me feel things I never thought possible.

"You're brave," he says simply, tracing my jawline with his thumb. "You faced me head-on, and you never backed down."

Slowly, I nod again, not sure what else to say. The praise catches me off guard, but it also feels right. He deserves the truth, even if it's hard to swallow.

"You're not so bad yourself," I manage to whisper, my voice barely above a whisper.

His lips quirk up in a small smile. "Flatterer." He pulls me back into his embrace, and we stay like that for a while longer, lost in our own thoughts.

Eventually, we hear footsteps approaching the door. Marco tenses, and I can feel the shift in his body language. He's all business now. "Get dressed," he commands.

I do as he says, pulling on my dress from earlier. It's now wrinkled and stained with sweat, a testament to our passionate encounter.

When I emerge from the bedroom, Marco is gone, leaving me with a lingering sense of awe and confusion. But also, an undeniable longing for more. This can't be happening... or maybe it's exactly how it should be.

I make my way downstairs on shaky legs, still feeling the aftereffects of Marco's skilled touch. My core throbs pleasantly with each step, and I have to bite my lip to stifle a moan.

In the foyer, Marco is barking orders at his men, clearly preparing for retaliation against the rival family that dared to attack us. His expression is stern, almost cruel, a far cry from the tender lover I knew only minutes ago.

He senses my presence and turns to face me, his gaze softening for the briefest moment. Then he's all business again.

"The security team will monitor the house. I have... matters to attend to." His jaw clenches, a muscle feathering in his cheek. "You will hear from me soon."

I swallow hard, acutely aware of the eyes on us. His men know we were intimate, and now they're watching to see how Marco handles me. Asserting control and dominance in front of them is clearly important.

Still, I can't help the flare of hurt in my chest. After everything we shared, he's dismissing me so easily. As if I mean nothing.

I lift my chin, refusing to show any weakness. Now is not the time to show him or his men how I really feel. "Of course, Signore De Luca. I understand you have a job to do."

The words taste bitter on my tongue, but I stand by them. This is the life I chose when I agreed to marry Marco, danger and unpredictability included. I knew what I was getting into.

If only my heart understood that too. In a way, I think it did at first. But the mind's stubbornness is no match for true love.

Marco's gaze sharpens, and for a moment I think he sees right through me. But then he gives a curt nod and turns away, already issuing new orders to his men.

I let out a shaky breath and head for the door, more uncertain of my place here than ever before.

I stare out the window at the swirling sea, lost in thought. So much has changed in such a short time. Barely a week ago, Marco and I were still uneasy strangers bound by an arranged marriage. Now we've shared an intimacy I never could've imagined, only to be plunged back into the brutal realities of his world.

It's foolish to wish for any normalcy or predictability here. I knew that going in, and yet part of me had hoped...

What? That Marco would sweep me off into the sunset, away from the violence and danger? I shake my head at my own naïveté. That will never be our story. If I'm going to find happiness with Marco, it will be in spite of the chaos, not separate from it.

The question is whether I have the strength for that. Whether our fledgling bond can endure the trials ahead.

My fingers curl into the throw rug folded over an arm of the couch, anxiety twisting in my gut. I think of Marco's searing kiss, the raw emotion in his voice as he confessed how I've come to mean everything to him, and the way he made rough but tender love to me. If that was real—and I believe it was—then we have a chance.

But we'll have to face each challenge together, guarding the fragile gift between us with everything we have. I close my eyes, summoning the memory of Marco's embrace and our intimacy to bolster my courage for the road ahead.

It won't be easy. But for a love like ours, I'm willing to fight. I only hope Marco feels the same. When next I see him, I'll make sure he understands I'm here to stay... if he'll have me.

I take a deep breath, realizing this marks my descent into an uncertain future. But not alone, never again alone. Marco and I will forge our path together, come what may.

Of that, at least, I'm sure.

Eleven

Alessia

I slide the brush across the canvas, blending the paints into a swirl of color. Painting is my escape, a small piece of the old me that still remains. Marco was kind enough to set up a room as my studio, rekindling a hobby I hadn't had much time for while running the café. I lose myself in the rhythm of each stroke, imagining I'm anywhere but here.

A knock at the door startles me from my thoughts. Strange, I'm not expecting anyone. Not hearing any of the staff answer the door, I figure they must be on their lunch break. Oh well, it would be nice to have some human interaction. It gets lonely during the day when Marco is at work and the staff are busy working.

I open the door to find two delivery men with a large package. I'm not expecting anything, but Marco and the staff have all kinds of things delivered throughout the day. As I sign for it, one of the men suddenly grabs me from behind. A cloth covers my mouth and I smell something chemical. I try to scream but only manage a muffled cry, and there's a burning in my lungs before everything goes dark.

When I come to, I'm in the back of a van speeding down the road. Fear courses through me as the reality of the situation sinks in. I've been kidnapped. Who has taken me? And where are they taking me? I struggle against the ties binding my wrists. The men pay me no attention, focused stoically on the road ahead.

My heartbeat pounds in my ears. I squeeze my eyes shut, willing this to be some terrible nightmare. But when I open them again, I'm still here. Trapped. I think of Marco and wonder if he even knows yet that I'm gone. A mix of panic and determination wells up inside me. I don't know why I've been taken, and clearly these men are dangerous, but I refuse to go down without a fight.

Marco

Chaos erupts the moment I enter the estate. Men are shouting, phones are ringing. Francesco grabs me, panic in his eyes.

"Boss! It's Alessia—she's been taken!"

His words hit me like a blow. Alessia, kidnapped? Impossible. I was just with her this morning, vowing to keep her safe. And the grounds are secure, equipped with the best security systems and security team money can buy.

"What?! When did this happen?" I demand.

"Just now. We found signs of a struggle near the front entrance. No one saw who did it. The cameras were somehow disabled. We think they may have come in a delivery truck. Our men are scouting the neighborhood and one neighbor thinks they saw a van coming up the driveway."

A mix of rage and fear courses through me. How could I let this happen? I swore to protect her.

My men look to me, awaiting orders. I force myself to focus. Now is not the time for emotion. Or to show weakness.

"Search the grounds again. Check the security footage. I want every inch of this place combed for clues. We must find her, and quickly."

My voice is steel but inside, my mind reels. Memories of Alessia flash through me—her smile, her spirit, the growing connection between us. A shiver runs down my spine as I think about the groups of men who may have taken her, none of them good options. If anything happens to her...

No. I cannot think like that. I will find her. And I will destroy whoever took her. No one steals from Marco De Luca. No one. And she is my most prized possession.

I storm into my office, barking orders as I go.

"Get all our contacts on the line. Call in every favor, follow every lead. I want her found now!"

My men scramble to obey. Phones are dialing, voices shouting. But my mind is racing ahead.

Who could have taken her? Most likely a rival family trying to get to me—the Di Gregorios, for one? No, they'd have demanded a ransom by now... or worse, they'd have sent proof of death to show me what they've done. I shiver. No, that can't be it. A personal vendetta then? Someone from her past? Another syndicate posturing for control?

Alessia has secrets, I know that much. Things she is reluctant to share. Everyone does. Is this connected? Has my world put her directly in harm's way? Or is it something that came about just by virtue of her family lineage.

The thought makes my gut twist. This is my fault. I swore to protect her, yet I'm the one who brought her into all this. What if she'd been just fine staying at the café? What if me and my men were the only ones interested in that location? I have no idea whether I've done the right thing or made things one million times worse.

Francesco enters, his face grim. "No ransom demand yet, boss. Should we put feelers out, let them know we're looking to negotiate?"

"No," I snap. "I won't play their games. Just find her so we can get her back safely. And then we'll make them pay."

He nods and leaves. I pour a scotch, trying to steady my nerves.

Where are you, Alessia? What are they doing to you? Bile rises in my throat as dark thoughts creep in.

Stay strong, I plead silently. I will find you. And heaven help those who took you when I do. The wrath of Marco De Luca will rain down on them until there is nothing left.

This I swear.

I nod to Francesco as he enters my office again, bracing myself for whatever news he brings.

"The Rosales cartel got in touch," he says. "They're the ones who took her."

My hands clench into fists. The Rosales. Of course. We've been battling over territory for months now. I suspected the Di Gregorios, but even they have some kind of moral code which would hopefully keep my wife off limits. The Rosales? They're a whole other story.

"What do they want?" I ask through gritted teeth.

Francesco hesitates. "They said they'll exchange her for control of the docks."

I slam my fist on the desk, making him jump. Control of the docks means control over all incoming shipments. It would cripple my entire operation.

But this is about more than business. This is about Alessia. My Alessia.

"They think they can use her against me?" I seethe. "That I'll hand my empire over to save some woman?"

Francesco shifts his weight. "Not some woman, boss. Your woman. Your wife."

I meet his gaze. Because he's right. Alessia is not just some woman. But I can't show that weakness, not even to my most trusted men.

"She knew the risks that came with me," I say coldly. "Just like we all do."

But inside, my heart is shattering. Alessia in the hands of the Rosales cartel, being hurt because of me. They're known for being particularly ruthless, and for using people to send very clear messages. Thinking about her in that situation... helpless, vulnerable... it's unbearable.

Still, I force myself to breathe steadily, my face an emotionless mask. This is the ugly business I'm in. And I cannot let it break me now.

I pace the floor of my office, my mind racing. Where would they take her? The Rosales have compounds throughout the city, any one of which could be holding Alessia now.

I think back to this morning, kissing her goodbye before my meeting. The way her eyes shone with that clever spark, how she teased me about my grumpiness before coffee. So full of life and spirit.

The thought of that light dimmed, her fire extinguished, makes my gut twist with fear and rage.

No. I cannot afford to think like that. Alessia is strong, stronger than she knows. She'll hold on until I find her.

And I will find her. I'll scour every inch of this damned city if I have to.

My cell phone rings, an unknown number. I answer quickly.

"Hello?"

There's silence on the other end, then muffled voices in the background. My heart leaps into my throat.

"Alessia?" I ask urgently. "Alessia, is that you?"

More silence, then finally, her voice. Smaller than I've ever heard it. "Marco..."

Just that one word, but it's her. Relief crashes over me. "Alessia, listen, I'm going to get you out of there. Just tell me where you are, give me something-"

The call ends abruptly. I stare at the phone, hands shaking. It was her. She's alive. But for how long? I must act quickly.

My relief fuels my determination even more. I bark orders to trace the number, monitor for another call. I don't care what the Rosales want in return. Nothing is off the table when it comes to getting Alessia back.

I failed to protect her once from the dangers of my world. I won't fail her again. *I'm coming for you, my love. Just hold on a little longer.*

I pace my office like a caged lion, waiting for any scrap of information on Alessia's whereabouts.

My men report that the brief call from her came from a burner phone, untraceable. Another dead end.

I sweep my arm across my desk in frustration, sending papers and books crashing to the floor. How can there be no clues, no trail to follow? I'm supposed to have eyes and ears across this entire city.

I hear a soft knock at the door. Luca steps in hesitantly, wary of my foul mood.

"What?" I snap.

"The Rosales just sent another message. They want to meet tonight to discuss terms."

"Terms?" I repeat in disgust. "They kidnap and hold Alessia hostage, and now they want to negotiate terms? There will be no terms except her safe return!"

Luca shifts his weight. "Marco...we have to be smart about this. They know you'll do anything to get Alessia back. We can't appear too desperate."

I step close to Luca, glaring down at him. "I don't care about appearances. I want her back with me by any means necessary."

He swallows but stands firm. "I know. We all do. But if we act rashly, she could end up hurt...or worse." His voice drops on those last words.

As much as I want to rage, I know Luca speaks the truth. If I charge in blindly, Alessia's life is at greater risk. But the thought of bargaining with those rats, of playing their games while Alessia suffers...it makes my blood boil.

"Set the meet for tonight," I concede through gritted teeth. "But they'll regret this, Luca. They'll regret the day they dared lay a hand on her."

My temper may be restrained for now, but once Alessia is safe, the Rosales syndicate will feel the full force of my wrath. They will learn what happens when you cross Marco De Luca and take what is most precious to him.

I nod to Luca and he steps away to make the arrangements, his shoulders tense with unease. I know he and the others think my feelings for Alessia have made me reckless, blinded me to the realities of our business. Perhaps they're right. But I can't change how I feel about her. From the moment I saw her fiery and kind spirit, she captivated me in a way no other woman has.

Now as I stare out the window into the darkness, imagining her out there scared and alone, emotion wells up in me that I've never experienced before. Guilt that I brought her into this violent world gnaws at me. I should have protected her, kept her far away from the depraved machinations of the mafia. But instead I selfishly bound her to me, wanting to possess that radiant light. And now it may be extinguished because of my carelessness.

I slam my fist against the wall, the pain barely registering. Anguish and helplessness war within me. I've always been in control, commanding others' fates. But now Alessia's life hangs by a thread and I'm powerless to save her. The thought of losing her is unbearable. She's become far more to me than a strategic marriage or entertainment. Somewhere along the way, she stole my heart.

And if she dies, a part of me will die with her. I swear on my life, I will get her back safely or rain down unholy hell on those responsible. Either way they're going to pay for this. This isn't over yet.

I take a deep breath, trying to steady my raging emotions. I cannot afford to lose control, not when Alessia's life is on the line.

My men watch me warily, unaccustomed to seeing their unflappable boss so volatile. I see doubt creeping into their eyes. But I cannot show weakness, not now.

"Any word from Hector yet?" I ask Rocco, my other most trusted captain besides Luca.

He shakes his head. "Nothing since the video ransom demand this morning. They're laying low."

I curse under my breath. Hector Rosales and his men must have gone to ground after sending their little message, knowing we'd be scouring the city for them. Cowards.

I think back to the chilling video Hector sent me after the last phone call, Alessia bound and gagged in a dark room, her eyes wide with fear. My blood still boils as I imagine his sneering face as he named his price for her safe return. As if I would ever bow to that snake.

No, Alessia's life is not a bargaining chip. And I will remind Hector of that fact forcefully and permanently once I find him.

I turn to my assembled men. "Fan out and shake down all of Hector's known associates, Someone out there knows where he's keeping her. Make it clear what will happen if they choose to protect him over themselves."

My men murmur their assent and quickly move to obey. As they file out, I add "And bring me Hector's head before this day is through."

Their hungry grins tell me Hector Rosales' hours are numbered. Good. Let him cower for now. Justice will come for him swift and merciless.

I move to the window, peering out into the night. I will find you, Alessia. And once you're safe, no one will ever dare threaten you again. I swear it.

Twelve

Marco

I sit alone in my study, the weight of Alessia's kidnapping bearing down on me like a physical force. My usually immaculate appearance is disheveled— my tie loosened, my shirt wrinkled, my hair mussed from running my hands through it in frustration. I'm the visual embodiment of inner turmoil. If my men see me now, they'll have appropriate cause for concern.

How could I have let this happen? The guilt threatens to crush me. I knew the dangers that came with my lifestyle, yet I still allowed an innocent like Alessia to be caught in the crosshairs. My selfishness has now put her life at risk. To think, I proposed a marriage of convenience to keep her safe, when it only ended up further endangering her.

I knew there was a risk it could backfire, but there was a time when a mafia boss' wife was automatically considered 'safe' from being a target. With the underworld heating up the way it has been lately, I guess times have well and truly changed.

I remember the first time I laid eyes on her, so full of light and warmth, a stark contrast to the cold darkness that permeates my world. Over time, her playful smiles and teasing banter slipped past my defenses. Before I realized, I craved her presence. She became my oasis of joy in this harsh desert.

And now, visions of her bright eyes dulled by fear haunt me. The thought of her kind spirit broken twists my gut. I never meant for this, never wanted the violence to touch her. But intentions mean nothing in the face of my damning choices.

My fists clench as I think of her at the mercy of my enemy. As a mafia boss, I'm used to making difficult decisions, dealing with constant danger. But it's different when someone innocent is involved, someone I've come to cherish.

Can I really continue on this path, now that I've seen the true cost? Or is it too late for me to change, to leave behind this life of violence and become someone worthy of Alessia's light? I don't have the answers, but I know one thing for certain—I will do whatever it takes to get her back safely. I swear it.

I pace the room, my mind racing through useless what-ifs and self-recriminations. What good is that now? I need to focus on how to get her back, on making this right somehow.

I stop at the window, images of our time together flashing through my mind. I remember the first time I saw her smile since she'd been staying here. She had tripped, scattering the books she carried across the villa's marble floors. As I helped her gather them, she laughed it off with an easy grace. Her smile lit up her whole face, warming me to my core. I had turned away gruffly, hiding my reaction. She brought light where there had previously only been darkness, injecting a reminder that life is about more than just business and ruthless decisions.

Another memory surfaces—her playing the piano, her slender fingers dancing across the keys as moonlight streamed over her. The haunting melody and her rapt focus drew me in. I had never heard anything so beautiful. And when, by chance or by fate, she played my mother's favorite sonata, my heart had almost burst. For the first time since I was a little boy, I felt a flicker of true joy.

In that moment, I realized how much I'd come to care for her. But the tenderness I felt was laced with fear. My enemies would use any vulnerability against me. I should have tried to push her out of my mind, to protect us both. Kept this to the strictly business arrangement I had always intended it to be. To protect her, and to preserve my own image.

Yet she persisted, refusing to let me retreat behind my walls. Quickly after moving in, she saw me as more than a ruthless mafia boss, more than violence and shadows. She saw the man I buried deep within and made me want to be him again. I found myself smiling, even laughing and joking, and our conversation flowed with ease. I've shared more with her than I have with anyone else. She knows me, and she still wants to be by my side. And now, look what has happened because of me.

I release a shaky breath, the memories fading. My chest aches, knowing I may have lost the chance for light she offered. But if there's any way I can make this right, can save her from the darkness I dragged her into, I have to try. I will find her, no matter the cost.

I stare out the window into the inky night, the city lights blurred through the rain streaking down the glass. The storm matches the one raging inside me since Alessia was taken. I should have known she'd be targeted because of her closeness to me, should have prepared for this. But I got complacent, let my guard down. Now she's paying the price for my failure.

I slam my fist against the wall, the sharp pain grounding me momentarily. I've endangered people before, but this feels different. With Alessia, I let her past my defenses in a way I've never allowed anyone else. Her inner light called to the humanity I'd locked away, made me want things I shouldn't.

But I can't change who I am, can't erase the blood staining my hands. My father groomed me as his heir, forged me into a ruthless leader who puts the family above all else. Emotion is a liability in this world. I learned that lesson early on.

Yet when I'm with Alessia, the code I've lived by starts to crack. I find myself wanting more than power and control. I want lazy mornings together, her head resting on my chest. I want the simple joy of making her laugh. I want breakfasts with her — cheese and ham croissants with fruit salads and coffee and freshly squeezed orange juice, vacations in bustling cities and lazy seaside towns and opulent mansions and bougie yurts, holiday celebrations with family and friends at our place and just by ourselves all over the world. I want to watch horror movies that make her squeal and snuggle up to me on the blanket. I want to watch comedy movies so hilarious that she laughs until she doubles over and squeals because her stomach and cheeks hurt. I want pets—cats, dogs, hell...maybe even some horses and chickens. And maybe... maybe even children one day. For the first time I can remember, I want a life beyond this empty mansion and the never-ending violence.

I pace the length of my office, my polished Oxfords clicking against the cold marble floor. This room usually provides comfort in its dark wood accents and familiar scents of aged whiskey and tobacco. Tonight, the shadows seem to mock me.

I pour myself a glass of 40-year Scotch, my hands trembling ever so slightly. The alcohol burns going down but does nothing to steady my thoughts.

I close my eyes, seeing her smile, hearing her whisper my name. I clench my fist, knowing what I have to do. The Family can't know of this weakness. As far as they're concerned, Alessia is just a pawn, leverage to use against our greatest rivals. I may be a mafia boss, but there's always someone higher up the food chain, even at my level. And they have no place in their business for something as foolish as love.

I will find her and end this. But after, I can't be what she needs. My world will only destroy her light. To protect her, I must let her go.

I think back to our first meeting at her little coffee shop. She refused to be intimidated by my tailored suit and permanent scowl. Her smile was sunlight breaking through the clouds, her laugh a melody I'd never heard before. I could tell she was scared, but the way she jutted out her jaw and stifled her fear, telling me where to go when I tried to close her café for a few weeks... I'll never forget her courage.

Being with her was like a drug, an escape from the ruthless world I inhabit. I found myself craving her company, spending long nights talking instead of working. She saw beyond the mythic mafia boss to the man I buried long ago.

Alessia's captivity is my fault. I never should have let things progress between us, never should have indulged the foreign yearning she stirred within me. My selfishness has put her in danger, all because I craved the warmth she radiated, like a moth drawn to her flame.

My hands clench into fists as I imagine what she must be enduring. Fear coils hot and tight in my gut. I've seen the lengths my rivals will go to for leverage. If they've hurt her...

Something savage and feral rises up in me. I want to tear them apart with my bare hands, make them suffer as she has suffered. The urge is a living thing, screaming for release.

With effort, I tamp it down. That's the old me talking, driven by rage instead of reason. I need to be cold, calculating. I will get her back, but I must be careful. One misstep could cost Alessia her life.

What have I become? I built my reputation on being ruthless, ready to sacrifice anyone for the good of the family. Now a sweet and beautiful café owner has brought one of the most powerful men in the city to his knees.

But men like me don't get happy endings. My father made sure I learned that lesson early. This life requires sacrifice and pain, the needs of the many outweighing those of the few. Or in this case, of one innocent woman.

I stare at the phone, knowing what I need to do. As much as it will haunt me, I have to cut ties with Alessia completely. If I can get her back unharmed, my love can only destroy her. Once she's safe, I will let her go, no matter how deeply it wounds us both.

Alessia, my sweet love, I hope one day you will understand and forgive me. I thought I could shelter you from the storms within me, but they have broken free of my control. You awoke something in me I can never have. Now all I can do is set you free. If it's not too late.

I sit alone in my dimly lit study, curtains drawn against the morning light. The ice in my tumbler has long since melted, the amber liquid largely untouched. My appearance is even more disheveled than before, the dark circles under my eyes betraying my sleepless night.

A soft knock at the door rouses me from my brooding. "Come in," I call out, my voice rough with exhaustion.

Luca enters cautiously. I've sequestered myself for hours by now, ever since getting the chilling news of Alessia's abduction. I can tell by the sympathetic look on his face that Luca's heart aches for me, knowing how deeply this has affected me.

"You look like hell," he says gently as he takes the seat across from me.

My mouth twitches in a humorless smile. "I thought you were supposed to tell the boss he looks great no matter what."

"Maybe for the others. But it's just me here." Luca studies my haggard face. "Talk to me, Marco. Let me help shoulder this burden."

I lean forward, dropping my head into my hands. "It's my fault, Luca," I say, voice thick with self-loathing. "I swore to protect her, but instead I brought this danger into her life."

I look up, anguish in my dark eyes. "She trusted me completely. All I've done is betray that trust over and over."

Luca hesitates, then asks the question no one else dares. "Do you.
..do you love her?"

I flinch at the word, like it's a bullet to my heart. For a long moment,
I just stare at the floor.

"I didn't mean to," I finally whisper. "But she found a way in,
despite all my walls. No one has gotten close to me in a long time,
Luca. I don't know how to protect someone I..." My voice trails off.

Luca nods in understanding. He knows me, perhaps better than
anyone. And he's never seen me like this—raw, vulnerable, stripped of
my usual stoic control.

"We'll get her back, Marco," Luca says firmly. "Whatever it takes. I
swear to you."

I pass a weary hand over my face. When I look up, my expression is
resolute. The ice has returned to my eyes. I can't let any of them see
behind the mask. Even Luca. I've already said too much.

"Yes we will. And then I have to let her go, for good this time." My
voice turns cold. "My world is no place for someone like her."

I stand abruptly, signaling an end to the conversation. Luca watches
me stride from the study, spine rigid, once again locked behind an
impenetrable wall. But despite my attempts to conceal it, Luca knows
the truth—my armor has been forever cracked open. There is no going
back from this.

Three days later

I turn at the sound of another soft knock. Luca enters, his expression grim. My men have scoured the city for days with no luck. It has been hell, pure torture sitting here waiting and wondering, dark thoughts swirling in my mind at what the heavy weight of silence means. Of what's happening to my darling Alessia as our attempts to find her prove futile. But finally, we might have a lead.

"The Rosales' are making a shipment out of the old lumber yard tonight," Luca says. "Rumor is, they're moving something important."

My eyes lock with his. It's not much, but it's our first real break. I feel the chess pieces moving into place in my mind. If I play this right, the king will fall. And I will have my queen back.

"Get the men ready," I tell Luca. "We're going to pay them a visit."

He nods and turns to go. At the door, he pauses, glancing back. "We're getting her home, Marco. Whatever it takes."

I meet his eyes and see the promise there. These men have been with me for years. They know what Alessia means to me now, as much as I've tried to hide it. Failure is not an option for any of us.

The game is on. No more waiting, just action. I feel the change in myself and I know my enemies will soon feel it too. There's a storm coming for them. And her name is Alessia.

I nod, the weight of what's to come pressing down on me. So much could still go wrong. If I've miscalculated...

I close my eyes, picturing Alessia's face. Her smile, lighting up a room. Her laughter, rare and musical. The way she looks at me, unafraid.

She believes I can be more than this. More than a ruthless monster. And for her, I thought maybe I could try.

But now she's paying the price for my foolish dream. Locked away somewhere, afraid. All because of the man I am.

I should never have let things go so far. I should have protected her from myself most of all.

Tomorrow, I make this right. I'll tear this city apart if I have to. I will find her. And I will bring her home.

After, if she still wants me, I'll spend my life making this up to her. I'll leave this darkness behind. I'll become the man she deserves.

But tonight, I need the monster one last time. To rip apart anyone who stands between us. No mercy this time. No more games.

A final reckoning is coming. My enemies wanted to ignite the fire inside of the devil? Tomorrow, I give them hell.

For you, Alessia, I will walk through fire. Just hold on a little longer. I'm coming.

Thirteen

Alessia

The cold concrete floor bites through my thin dress as I wake. I blink in the harsh fluorescent lights of a tiny room. A bare mattress, a toilet, a sink—what appears to be my new home. A temporary one, I hope. It feels like whiplash, going from my cramped apartment to Marco's palatial villa, and now to this tiny, unrecognizable space. I've never been to jail before, but I imagine it looks a lot like this. The heavy metal door clangs open and a hulking guard steps in, face obscured by a black mask.

"On your feet," he barks. I shiver at the sound of his voice and stand slowly, steadying myself. I have no idea who this man is or what they want from me. But I won't show weakness, won't give them the satisfaction. The guard shoves a tray of food at me and slams the door shut.

Alone again, I sink to the floor and take a deep breath. I have to keep it together, stay sharp. My gut tells me that Marco will find me. But I can't rely on him. I'm not the naive cafe owner I was a week ago. If I want to get out of this alive, I need to use every bit of wit and grit I have. My own deep mafia roots must count for something, some kind of latent DNA that makes me good at being cunning and conniving like my ancestors before me.

I scan the room, cataloging potential weapons and weak spots. I've watched enough action movies to know what to look for. One of the eating utensils could be sharpened into a shiv, and the hinges on the door look old. I'll bide my time and gather anything useful—a stray nail, a piece of glass. And I'll watch the guards closely, learn their routines, and look for any lapse in vigilance. No matter how long it takes me, I'm determined to get out of here.

I choke down the stale bread and watery soup, fueled by determination. I will get out of this hell. I will see Marco again. I will see my grandmother and my café again. I cling to Marco's face in my mind—the warmth of his smile, his intense, brooding eyes. The thought of him steadies me. I just have to survive one moment at a time.

I pocket the spoon from my meal. It's not much, but it's a start. As the hours drag on in isolation, my thoughts drift back to Marco. I never wanted this criminal life, but now I'm in the thick of it. Marco tried to protect me, but I'm not some damsel. I've found reserves of courage I didn't know I had.

When we first met, I thought Marco was just another mobster thug. But he saw more in me—he quickly came to appreciate my spirit, my kindness. He opened up to me in a way he never has with anyone else.

I fell for the man behind the mafia boss persona, his inner depths and softness visible only to me.

And now here I am—kidnapped, caged like an animal. But I refuse to break. Marco showed me my own strength, believing I could handle the truth about his dark world. Now I understand what he meant. My love for Marco has transformed me. I know that within I'm cunning, relentless, fearless. Traits I'll need to get out of this alive.

The door creaks open and I slip the spoon into my sleeve. The same hulking guard enters with another tray. As he turns his back, I make my move, striking him hard behind the knees. He crumples and I sprint for the door, bursting into a dingy hallway. Freedom awaits, if I can just make it outside.

The guard's shouts echo behind me as I race down the corridor. My bare feet slap against the cold concrete floor. I have no idea where I'm going, relying on instinct alone. All that matters is escape.

I round a corner and nearly collide with another guard. He grabs for me but I duck and keep running, my breath coming in ragged gasps. The hallway seems to go on forever, each locked door a dead end. I groan with despair each time I unsuccessfully tug on an unbudging handle.

Finally I come to a stairwell. Taking the steps two at a time, I emerge into a cavernous room filled with packing crates. A large bay door stands slightly ajar, sunlight streaming through the opening. My heart leaps—I'm so close.

I sprint for the exit, weaving between stacks of crates. The bay door is just ahead when suddenly two guards step into view, blocking my path. I skid to a stop, trapped.

The men advance toward me, cruel smiles on their faces. Adrenaline surges through my veins. I'm not going back without a fight. And it's like every self defense class I've ever taken is suddenly clicking into place, like I'm an unhinged *American Ninja Warrior*. Nothing can stop me. Grabbing a loose plank of wood, I swing with all my might. The makeshift weapon connects with a satisfying crack. One guard drops like a stone.

His partner lunges but I sidestep, bringing the plank down hard on his back. He crumples with a howl of pain. I leap over his body and make one final dash for freedom, throwing my weight against the metal door. It gives way and I tumble outside into blinding sunlight, gulping the fresh air.

I made it. Battered and breathless, but free. This is just the beginning though. Now to get back to Marco. Back to the man I love.

I take a moment to get my bearings and calm my racing heart. The area around me looks to be some kind of industrial yard or shipping facility. Stacks of containers and heavy machinery surround the warehouse I just escaped from.

In the distance I can see a main road, the promise of civilization. But between me and it sprawls a maze of buildings and equipment. I'll have to navigate carefully to avoid running into more of my captors.

Picking a direction, I start making my way through the complex. The midday sun beats down as I creep from cover to cover. It's eerily quiet. Where is everyone? Surely word has gotten out by now that I've escaped.

The sound of approaching engines shatters the stillness. I duck behind a bulldozer just as two black SUVs roar into view. The vehicles screech to a stop near the building I fled from.

Angry shouts arise as men pour out and find their incapacitated comrades. My heart sinks. They definitely know I've escaped by now. It's only a matter of time before they come looking.

I can't stay here. Keeping low, I sprint toward a stack of containers, looking for a place to hide. Their voices fade as I worm my way deep into the metallic maze. It's cooler here, but stifling.

Wedging myself between two containers, I try to control my breathing. I just need to stay hidden until nightfall. Then maybe I can slip away under the cover of darkness. I still feel exposed, so I make my way between the containers until I finally find an entrance into one of them. As I clamber through I gag. It smells like rotting flesh, the decay of what I hope are animal corpses but fear are actually human. I have no doubt that these men, whoever they are, are well-equipped for a human trafficking operation. And that industry is known for its tragedies.

One way or another, I will get back to Marco. I replay our last moment together in my mind—his lips crushing mine in a desperate kiss. The promise we made to each other. I cling to that memory like a lifeline, determined to survive. For him. For us.

I don't know how much time has passed curled up in this metal coffin. Minutes? Hours? My legs ache from crouching, but I don't dare move. Any noise could give me away.

Muffled voices drift through the containers, sending adrenaline coursing through my veins. I squeeze my eyes shut, willing them to pass by.

The heavy footfalls grow louder. They're close. Too close. I stop breathing, listening intently as they approach my hiding spot.

This is it. I brace myself, ready to fight. A loud clang makes me flinch. But it came from farther away—they're throwing open container doors, one by one.

My heart hammers against my ribs. I can't stay trapped like a rat. As their search nears, I slip out and creep along the edge of the container stack.

Up ahead, a dark gap between two stacks beckons. I move toward it just as a shout goes up behind me. They've spotted me. *Shit.*

I bolt for the opening, but skid to a halt—it's a dead end. Wheeling around, I see them charging straight for me, guns raised. Nowhere to run.

I back up against the containers, sizing up my pursuers. No more hiding. If I'm going down, it won't be without a fight. With a primal cry, I charge into the fray.

I barrel into the first man, driving my shoulder into his gut. He doubles over with a grunt as I rip the gun from his hands, suddenly grateful for the self defense classes my grandmother insisted I take when I was growing up. There's no time to aim—I swing it like a club against his temple. He collapses as he cries out in agony.

The others close in, shouting threats in what I recognize as Spanish. One grabs at me—I smash the gun into his face then kick hard at his knee. A sickening crack, and he crumples with a scream.

Two left. The biggest one charges, trying to tackle me. I sidestep, bringing the gun down on the back of his head. He faceplants into the asphalt.

The last man hesitates, eyeing his fallen comrades. Our eyes lock—his dark and venomous, mine blazing with adrenaline. In a heartbeat, he turns and runs.

My chest heaves as I watch him flee. The urge to give chase courses through me, but I know I can't stop now. Freedom is so close.

I drop the dented gun and sprint on, weaving between the maze of containers. Just ahead, the stacked rows give way to a tall chainlink fence—the perimeter. Freedom.

I scramble up and over, ignoring the bite of metal in my palms. As I drop to the ground on the other side, a burst of elation surges through me. I made it. I'm free.

But my relief is short-lived. Headlights flash at the far end of the shipping yard, followed by shouting. Reinforcements. Of course an operation as sophisticated as this would have a larger team.

I steel myself and run on. The fight for my life isn't over yet.

I take off into the night, my feet pounding on the cracked pavement. The shipping yard gives way to empty streets and shuttered warehouses. I don't know where I'm going, only that I need to get as far away as I can.

Glancing back, I see the headlights in the distance as my captors' men sweep the area looking for me. My lungs burn and my legs ache, but I push myself harder. I can't let them catch me again.

As I round a corner, the streets open up into a more populated area. Nightclubs and bars line the sidewalks, with groups of partygoers laughing and chatting outside. Civilization. I slow to a brisk walk, trying to blend into the crowds.

I feel exposed and vulnerable, but there's safety in numbers. I weave my way through the busy streets, keeping my head down. The sounds of the city surround me—music pulsing from club entrances, raucous laughter, honking horns. But all I can focus on is the pounding of my heart.

I'm so close to getting away, to my freedom, but I know the danger isn't over. The reach of Marco's enemies is long and their wrath endless. They won't stop until they take him down, which now includes finding me. He suggested this arrangement to save me, but it seems like my family background means I'm screwed either way.

As I pass by an alley, a black sedan screeches to a halt in front of me, blocking my path. My blood turns to ice. I turn to flee in the opposite direction, but it's too late. My captors' men jump out, grabbing at me. I twist and fight, but there are too many of them. A needle pricks my neck and my limbs go heavy. The world spins and fades to black.

When I come to, I'm in the back of the sedan, my hands bound. My head feels heavy and it's hard to keep my eyes open. We're speeding through the city, streetlights flashing by in a blur. Despair crashes over me. I was so close, but now I'm right back where I started. A prisoner of an unknown rival.

But as we drive on into the night, a tiny flicker of defiance still burns inside me. I won't give up. One way or another, I will have my freedom. Whoever has taken me can't keep me chained forever. And I will find my way back to Marco.

Fourteen

Alessia

The compound explodes into chaos as the door blows open. Marco's men swarm inside, guns blazing. I crouch behind the overturned table, my pulse racing. Relief surges through my body as I realize they're here to rescue me, although I recognize things are far from over yet. Boots pound across the concrete floor. Bullets zing past. I squeeze my eyes shut, willing it to be over.

"Alessia!" A familiar voice shouts my name. Rocco. I peer over the edge of the table. Rocco strides toward me, his face streaked with blood and grime, his eyes burning with determination. He reaches for my hand to pull me up.

That's when the gunshot splits the air.

Rocco's body jerks, a blossom of red spreading across his chest. His mouth forms a surprised O shape as he crumples to the ground.

I scream, frozen in horror. Men shout and scramble around us. Rocco's blank eyes stare at nothing. Bile rises in my throat. After everything, he died to save me.

A firm hand grasps my shoulder. "We have to move, now!" Marco's lieutenant urges. I take one last look at Rocco's body, grief and guilt twisting my gut. It feels wrong leaving him here like this, but we have no choice. Then I let the lieutenant guide me outside into blazing sunlight, the taste of freedom tainted by death.

Marco is waiting by the idling cars, his men forming a protective circle around him. His head snaps up as we emerge from the compound. Relief floods his eyes, quickly replaced by concern as he takes in my disheveled state.

"Alessia," he breathes, stepping toward me. I flinch involuntarily at his sudden movement. Marco's face darkens. "What did they do to you?" he growls.

I shake my head, unable to speak. The past few days crash over me—the terror, the isolation, Rocco's lifeless eyes. My legs give out and I sink to my knees, ragged sobs tearing from my throat.

Marco kneels and pulls me against his chest, enveloping me in his warmth and familiar scent. "Shh, I've got you now. You're safe," he murmurs into my hair.

I cling to him, the dam broken. All the fear and trauma pour out of me. Marco's strong arms support me, his hand stroking my back gently. He whispers soothing words in Italian as I soak his shirt with tears.

Gradually my sobs subside to hiccups. Marco tilts my chin up, his eyes roving my face. I must look a mess—bruises, scratches, tangled hair, dirt-smudged skin. His jaw tightens as he takes in each mark marring my skin.

"I'll make them pay for this," he vows darkly.

I shake my head again, too exhausted for vengeance. "Just take me home," I whisper.

Marco presses a fierce kiss to my forehead. "Let's go home." Despite his acquiescence, I can tell its not over yet. But for now, retribution can wait.

He helps me to my feet, keeping an arm around my waist as he leads me to the waiting car. I sag against him, the fight drained out of me. But with Marco at my side, I feel a flicker of hope again. We've been through hell, but we survived. Together.

Marco helps me into the backseat of the sleek black car. I sink into the plush leather, comforted by the familiarity of it, the scent of Marco's familiar aftershave permeated every corner. This is Marco's car, his world. A world I thought I might never see again.

As Marco slides in next to me, I study his face. The lines around his eyes are deeper, his mouth set in a grim line. But his eyes soften when they meet mine. He's so very handsome, even when he's exhausted. He brushes a strand of hair from my face gently.

"How are you feeling?" he asks.

I let out a shaky breath. "Honestly? Like I've been hit by a truck. Everything hurts. I'm exhausted."

Marco nods, his jaw tightening again. "I'm so sorry, Alessia. I should have protected you better."

"It's not your fault," I say, taking his hand in mine.

We sit in silence for a few moments. So much has happened, it's hard to process it all. The kidnapping, the beatings, wondering if each day would be my last. And now here I am, safe with Marco again. It almost doesn't feel real.

"I thought I'd never see you again," I confess in a small voice.

Marco squeezes my hand. "I wasn't going to stop until I found you. I would have torn the city apart if I had to."

I know it's true. Marco's loyalty and determination are unmatched. Still, the danger he put himself in to rescue me leaves me uneasy.

"Promise me you won't take risks like that again," I say.

Marco hesitates before answering. "I can't make that promise. Not if it means losing you."

"Your life is too important," I insist, meeting his dark gaze.

Something shifts between us in that moment. We both recognize the depth of our connection, how essential we've become to each other. The willingness we both have to put each other before ourselves. To risk our lives for each other. Marco pulls me against his side, pressing a kiss to the top of my head.

"We'll talk more when you've rested," he says gently. "For now, let's just get you home."

I nod, comforted by his solid presence. Whatever comes next, we'll face it together. The kidnapping has changed things between us. We're bound now, two lives forged into one by adversity. And nothing will tear us apart again.

Back at Marco's lavish mansion, I sink onto the plush sofa, exhausted. Marco sits beside me, his jaw clenched as he takes in the cuts and bruises marring my skin.

"I'm so sorry this happened to you," he says gruffly. "If it wasn't for me..."

He trails off, but I know what he's thinking. That his life in the mafia is what put me in danger.

"It's not your fault," I say, taking his hand. "My family roots played a part in this too. If I wasn't here with you, they would have come for me anyway. It was only a matter of time."

Marco shakes his head. "Yes, it is my fault. You got caught in the crossfire of my enemies trying to hurt me. And it could happen again."

His dark eyes are tormented. I know how heavily the burden of being the mafia boss weighs on him. He never wanted this violent life, but was born into it out of duty to his family. Something my own family sheltered me from until it inevitably caught up with me like a ghost from the past.

"Things have to change," Marco says finally. "I can't risk losing you again."

My breath catches at the gravity in his tone. "What are you saying?"

Marco takes a deep breath. "I'm saying it's time for me to walk away. From the mafia, from everything. The only life I want is one with you, Alessia."

I'm stunned into silence. The mafia is all Marco has ever known. And now he's willing to leave it all behind for me. It's the most selfless, romantic thing he could do.

"But what about your family? Your men?" I ask softly. "Everything you've ever worked for? Your family legacy?"

Pain flickers in Marco's eyes. "It won't be easy. But you're my family now too. I have to protect what matters most."

Overwhelmed, I throw my arms around Marco's neck. He holds me close as I finally let the tears fall, tears of relief that this nightmare is over. Marco presses a fierce kiss to my hair.

"I love you," he whispers. "We'll get through this, I swear it."

And I believe him with all my heart. Marco is giving up his empire for me. Now it's my turn to stand strong beside him on the difficult road ahead. Whatever comes, we'll face it together.

Marco

I take a deep breath and step forward to address my men directly.

"I've brought you here today because there's something important I need to say."

My voice echoes through the warehouse, all eyes fixed on me. This is the moment of truth.

"For ten years, I've led this family. We've accomplished things people said were impossible—taken on other families, seized power, and built a name for ourselves."

I pause, seeing the pride in their faces.

"But in doing so, we've all made sacrifices. The life we lead comes with a cost, as we've seen too many times." Rocco's face flashes in my mind, and I wince, just one of the loyal soldiers lost to this endless war.

"I can't in good conscience continue to ask that sacrifice of you, when I'm no longer willing to make it myself."

Murmurs ripple through the men. I steel myself and continue.

"Because of this life, I nearly lost someone irreplaceable to me. I won't risk that again. From today on, I'm stepping down as your boss."

Shouts of protest erupt, but I raise my hand for silence.

I knew telling the rest of the family about my decision to leave the mafia wouldn't be easy, but I wasn't prepared for the level of backlash I'm receiving.

My uncle Enzo is the first to react, slamming his fist on the table in anger. "You can't just walk away from this life," he spits. "Your father built this empire with his blood and sweat. You have a duty to this family."

I hold his fiery gaze steadily. "My only duty now is to Alessia. I won't risk her life anymore."

"Love makes you weak," Enzo sneers. "Our rivals will see this as a chance to destroy us. Without you at the head, we'll be ripped apart."

"My mind is made up. Nothing is more important than the woman I love. I won't lose her to this world of violence and fear. I know many of you depend on me, and for that I'm sorry. But it's time for me to leave the mafia behind."

I scan their stunned faces. "The family will go on without me. There are good, loyal men here who can lead you. I trust you'll make the right choices."

Around the table, I see others nod grimly. My cousin Vincenzo looks troubled but doesn't speak up. He knows as well as I do how dangerous our world can be.

"I don't have a choice," I say firmly. "I can't be the man Alessia needs and run the family too. This life put her in danger—that's not something I can allow again."

Enzo's eyes blaze, but before he can respond, my uncle Salvatore raises a hand. "Marco is right. There are some things more important than power or money. If you truly love this woman, she must come first."

I feel a rush of gratitude toward Salvatore. He's always been a voice of wisdom in our volatile family, and under his rough exterior he's a hopeless romantic.

"There will be consequences," Enzo says darkly. "Rivals like the Di Gregorios won't hesitate to strike against us. The Rosales' will almost certainly hit us again soon. The O'Malleys are always lying in wait just around the corner, those Irish punks. Your love may bring about the ruin of everything we've built!"

I meet Enzo's accusing glare steadily. "Then we'll face those consequences when they come. But I won't sacrifice the woman I love anymore."

I can see the dismay on the faces of my men. They've depended on me to lead them for so long. But though it pains me, I know I had to break free of this life that has caused so much suffering already. The challenges ahead will be immense, no matter what. But with Alessia by my side, I'm ready to face them.

With that, I turn and walk away, my heart pounding. The deed is done. Right or wrong, my old life ends today. A new uncertain future lies ahead, but with Alessia, I can face anything.

Alessia

Marco's words echo in my mind as I stare at him in disbelief. He's really doing it—leaving everything behind for me. After all we've suffered, I should feel only joy, but a knot of anxiety twists in my gut.

"Alessia, say something," Marco pleads, his eyes searching mine.

"I just...I can't believe it," I stammer. "You would give up your empire for me?"

Marco steps closer, taking my hands in his. "You're all that matters to me now. I was a fool not to see that sooner."

My heart swells, even as my mind spins with doubts. "But the mafia is your legacy, your family's honor. And it won't be easy to walk away."

"None of that is worth losing you," Marco says fervently. "We'll face whatever comes together."

I want to believe we could leave it all behind. But the dark world we've known doesn't release its grip so easily.

"I'm scared," I whisper. "Your rivals, even some of your own men. ..they won't let you go without a fight."

Marco's jaw tightens, his eyes hardening. "Let them come. I'll do whatever it takes to protect you, Alessia."

I cling to him then, tears filling my eyes. Marco has risked everything for me. Now it's my turn to be strong, to stand beside him no matter what the future holds. This is our chance at a new life. And I will fight for it with all I have.

Finally, I nod, holding back my doubts. This is our chance, I have to believe that.

We leave the gathering hand in hand, Marco's men parting to let us through. Their faces are grave, some angry, others confused. Word will spread quickly about Marco's decision.

Outside, his sleek black car idles at the curb. Marco opens the door for me, his eyes constantly scanning our surroundings. My heart is in my throat as I get in, feeling exposed and vulnerable.

The engine purrs to life, and we pull away into the night. Street-lights flash across Marco's stoic face as we drive in silence. I can feel the tension radiating from him. This goes against everything he's been raised for, betraying his father's legacy.

"Where will we go?" I ask softly.

"Somewhere far from here," Marco says, his knuckles white on the steering wheel. "I have a safe house prepared out west. We'll lie low until things settle down."

I shiver, hugging myself. The full weight of what we've done is sinking in. Marco has burned all his bridges for me. There's no going back now.

We'll have to watch our backs at every turn, constantly wary of threats from Marco's enemies. And from those to whom my parents owed a family debt that their rivals now intend to collect. Perhaps we'll never fully escape this life we were both born into, the bloody roots that run too deep.

But we have each other now. And for better or worse, our fates are intertwined.

Fifteen

Marco

L uca corners me in my study, a grim set to his jaw. "We need to talk."

I sigh, gesturing for him to sit. "What is it now?"

"The Rosales family," he says bluntly. "They're making moves again. Attacking our shipments, threatening our allies. They won't stop until they've taken over, Marco, or until we wipe them out. You saw what they did to Alessia. And you know they're not going to stop chasing you both down until we take them out completely. I need your help. This can't be my first task in your old role."

My stomach clenches. I've given up that life, left the mafia behind for Alessia. But Luca's right—the Rosales won't stop hounding us until they've destroyed what our family built.

"I'm stepping up as boss," Luca says, anxiety written across his face. "But I need your help to finish this once and for all. One last favor, Marco, that's all I ask."

One last favor. I close my eyes, thinking of Alessia's smile, her laughter, the life we've started to build. If I do this, that life will be stained with blood. But if I don't, she'll never be safe. The Rosales will use her again to get to me.

When I open my eyes, Luca's watching me closely. "You'll do it," he says with certainty. "For her, and for us. Family first, Marco. Always."

I set my jaw and meet his gaze. "One last favor," I echo. "But when this is done, I'm out. For good this time."

Luca nods. "Whatever you need to do to keep her safe. I understand." He stands, clasping my shoulder. "Meet me tonight to plan the attack. It's time to end this war once and for all."

As Luca leaves, dread and determination war inside me. I'm going back to the life I fled, the violence I abhor—all to protect the woman I love. Once the Rosales are defeated, we'll finally have peace. But at what cost? I can only pray Alessia will forgive me for the blood I'm about to spill.

I find Alessia in her art studio, sunlight filtering through the windows to illuminate her canvas. She's frowning at the half-finished painting, a swirl of dark colors and sharp edges that reflect the turmoil of our lives lately.

When she sees me, her expression softens. "You're back." She sets down her brush and wipes her hands, crossing the room to wrap me in her arms. "Did Luca convince you?"

I hold her close, breathing in her scent. "He did. It's the only way to end this, tesoro. But when it's over—"

"I know." She pulls back to meet my gaze. "When it's over, we're free. No more looking over our shoulders, no more threats. Just us, Marco, the way it was meant to be."

Her faith in our future steadies me. I cup her face in my hands, tracing the line of her jaw with my thumb. "Luca and I have a plan to ambush them tonight. If all goes well, the Rosales family will be defeated by dawn."

Alessia searches my eyes. "Promise me you'll be careful. I can't lose you, Marco, not when we've come this far."

"I promise." I kiss her softly. "After tonight, all of this will be behind us. We'll finally have the life we deserve."

She smiles, though worry still lingers in her gaze. "Go do what you have to do. I'll be here waiting for you when it's over."

I squeeze her hands before releasing them. Tonight will be dangerous, but the thought of coming home to Alessia keeps my steps steady as I leave to prepare. After so much darkness, our future is finally in sight. No matter the cost, I'll make sure we reach it—together.

I make my way through the empty streets, the familiar weight of my gun a grim comfort at my side. My men are waiting at our headquarters, preparing for the confrontation ahead. But first, there are allies I need to secure, men who still owe me their loyalty despite walking away from this life.

The door of the small café creaks open, a bell tinkling above. The owner, Bruno, looks up from wiping down the counter and nods in greeting. "Was wondering when you'd show up."

"We have unfinished business with the Rosales family," I say, sliding onto a stool. "I'm here to call in that favor you owe me."

Bruno's jaw tightens, his eyes flickering away. "Marco, you know I'm out of that life now. I can't—"

"Without our help, your brother would be dead. I saved your family, and now I'm asking you to return the favor." I lean forward, lowering my voice. "One last job, Bruno. Help me take down the Rosales, and your debt will be repaid. Then we can both leave this life for good. I promise."

He exhales heavily, dragging a hand over his face. "You drive a hard bargain. But I owe you too much to refuse." Bruno looks up, resignation and regret in his eyes. "What do you need?"

"Men. As many as you can spare. We attack at midnight."

Bruno gives a sharp nod. "Consider it done."

I clasp his shoulder, a silent thanks passing between us. My next stop is an auto shop downtown, one of my most lucrative fronts. The owner, Gianni, was once my right-hand man, as loyal as family. But he too walked away from this life, tired of the violence and chaos. Still, there are bonds that endure beyond this world—and Gianni owes me his allegiance.

Tonight, I'll call in the last of the favors I'm owed. Luca and I have a plan, but we'll need all the help we can get. The Rosales won't go down without a fight, and if we fail—there will be no future for me and Alessia. No escape from this life that has taken everything from us both.

The cost of victory will be high. But defeat is not an option. Not when we've finally glimpsed our future, not when freedom is so close I can almost taste it. Tonight, the Rosales era ends. And with the dawn, a new life begins.

Midnight. The old shipping yard is eerily empty, moonlight glinting off rusting metal and shattered glass. My men are in position, stationed throughout the dilapidated buildings and behind crumbling cargo containers. Luca and Gianni flank me, a grim anticipation etched into their features.

And behind them, Alessia. She insisted on coming, even though I warned her of how dangerous it would be. "You might distract me," I had told her. "I need all of my focus on taking out Rosales." "We are a team," she had replied "We went into this together, and we're coming out of it together." I had begrudgingly agreed, startled by her bravery even though I know she contains an inner strength that never fails to amaze me.

In my pocket is a single bullet. One way or another, this ends tonight.

The minutes tick by. My muscles are coiled tight, senses straining for any sign of movement. Then a flicker of light in the distance—the beam of a flashlight cutting through the darkness. I nod to Luca and my men fan out, melting into the shadows as a dozen figures emerge from the gates.

Rosales soldiers. And at their head, the snake himself—Hector Rosales.

They walk into the trap unknowing, confident in the territory they control. They thought I was done for good, not hunting them from the shadows. In the solitude of this place, there are no witnesses. No one to hear the gunshots that will ring out, or the cries of the dying.

My finger tightens around the trigger, every fiber of my being screaming to put a bullet in Rosales' head. But I hold steady, waiting for the right moment.

"Well, well," Rosales calls out, his mocking tone grating. "The infamous Marco De Luca. To what do we owe the pleasure?"

I step forward, standing in a pool of light. A challenge and a dare. "Your attempt to rain terror down on this city ends tonight."

Rosales laughs, the sound echoing through the yard. "Big words. Let's see if you can back them up." His men fan out, mirroring mine as a tense standoff ensues. The calm before the storm.

In this moment, I see it all with stark clarity—the violence that has shaped me, the love that saved me, the life I'm leaving behind. I tighten my grip on the gun, steeling myself for what comes next. For Alessia. For the future that awaits us.

I meet Rosales' gaze, a grim promise in my eyes. "I mean it, Hector. It ends tonight."

The first shot rings out. And all hell breaks loose.

Bullets whiz past, a hail of gunfire from both sides. My men take cover, returning fire as Rosales' men do the same. But I stand motionless, waiting. Watching.

There. A flash of movement to my left. One of Rosales' men emerges, taking aim. Before he can fire, a sharp crack rings out. He crumples with a cry, a bullet hole in his forehead.

I glance over to see Alessia lowering her gun, a steely glint in her eyes. She's found her target.

A surge of pride and fear wars within me. I want to shout at her to take cover, to get to safety. But I know she won't listen. Not when there are lives at stake. Not when this fight is as much hers as it is mine.

She's no longer the woman I met months ago, cowering in her gilded cage. The Alessia by my side is a force to be reckoned with—my partner in crime, my wife, the one person I know I can always count on.

Together, we stride into the fray, coordinating our shots to pick off Rosales' men one by one. The odds are still against us, but with Alessia at my side, I know we'll win this. We'll build the future we deserve, one bullet at a time.

Rosales snarls, realizing his forces are dropping like flies. He ducks behind a pile of crates, no doubt plotting his next move. But he won't get the chance.

I catch Alessia's eye and nod. It's time to end this.

We fan out, flanking Rosales on both sides. He emerges with a roar, guns blazing—only to falter at the sight of our guns trained on him.

Checkmate.

Rosales' eyes dart between us, rage and disbelief twisting his features. He opens his mouth for one final taunt—

Two shots ring out in unison. Rosales crashes to the ground, a bullet in his head and heart.

Silence falls over the yard as the last of the gunfire dies out. Then cheers erupt from my men, echoing into the night. The tyrant is dead. The day is won.

I pull Alessia into my arms, cradling her close. She's real and alive and mine. "It's over," I whisper, emotion choking my voice.

Alessia smiles up at me, fierce and bright. "No," she says softly. "It's just beginning."

She's right. Our future is just beginning. And this time, we'll face it together.

The yard is a mess of bodies and bullet casings, stark evidence of the violence that just unfolded. But in this moment, all I can see is Alessia.

She's illuminated in the pale moonlight, her cheeks flushed and her eyes shining with triumph. Gone is the shy, uncertain woman who first showed up at my mansion. In her place stands a queen, radiating strength and power. She's in her element amongst me and my men the same way she thrived back at her café.

No doubt the mafia world will be singing songs of our victory tonight. But they'll never understand what truly happened here.

Tonight, the old codes of honor and power struggles fell away. Tonight, love triumphed over hate. And from the ashes, a new era will rise.

An era where family is bound not by blood, but by choice. Where trust and devotion are given freely, not demanded through fear and force.

"It's really over, isn't it?" Alessia whispers, her hands coming to rest on my chest.

I pull her closer, relishing her warmth. "Yes, amore mio. The danger has passed."

Her lips curve into a soft smile and she shakes her head. "Not the danger. The old ways. We're free now...free to live the life we want. Together."

Joy and wonder swell within me at her words. She's right—we've been fighting for freedom in more ways than one. Freedom to love each other openly. Freedom to leave this life of crime behind. Freedom to choose our own path.

I cup Alessia's face in my hands, gazing into her eyes. The eyes I've lost myself in so many times. The eyes that reflect my very soul.

"The old ways are dead," I say firmly. "Long live the new."

Then I bring my lips to hers, sealing the promise with a kiss. Our future is ours to write—and this is only the beginning.

I pull back from the kiss, smoothing a stray hair from Alessia's face. Her cheeks are flushed, her lips kiss-swollen. She's never looked more beautiful.

"We should go," I say reluctantly. "There are still loose ends to tie up, and the authorities will be here soon."

Alessia nods, her expression turning serious once more. "You're right. We have a long road ahead." She bites her lip, glancing away. "Do you really think your men will follow you into this new life?"

"Not all of them." I sigh, the bitter truth settling over me. "But those who matter most understand why this change must come. The rest...they will fall in line or be left behind."

"I don't want you to lose people who are loyal to you because of me," she says quietly. Her mouth turns downward. "You already lost Rocco..."

I tilt her chin up, forcing her to meet my gaze. "I'm not losing anyone because of you. I'm finally doing what is right—for myself and for those who have suffered for too long under men like Rosales. You've opened my eyes to what this life should be." I brush my thumb over her lower lip. "And those who see the truth will stand with us. The rest be damned."

Alessia smiles, slow and sweet, and rises onto her toes to kiss me again. When she pulls back, her eyes are bright with purpose.

"Then let's go tie up those loose ends," she says, fierce determination etched into every line of her delicate features, "and start building the future we deserve."

I lace my fingers through hers, gripping tight. Together, we turn and walk away from the ruin of the old world we left behind.

Ready to face the new one waiting ahead.

We step out of the dingy warehouse, into the cool night air. It's a new beginning for us, a chance to leave our pasts behind and start anew. I lean down and whisper against her ear, "What do you want for our first night as retired mafia leaders?"

Her answer surprises me, thrills me. "Take me somewhere private," she breathes. "And teach me how to please you."

My heart thunders in my chest at her words. This woman, who once saw herself as weak and powerless, is transforming before my eyes. Tonight, she embraced her mafia roots, claiming her place beside me with an intensity that takes my breath away.

I lead her through the backstreets of the city, to the rooftop of an abandoned building with an unobstructed view of the stars. I lay her gently on a pile of old blankets, watching as she stares up at the sky, entranced. Gently, I begin to undress her. Her body is soft and warm beneath my touch, her gasps of anticipation filling the air.

"You're beautiful," I murmur against her skin. "Every inch of you."

She shivers as I kiss my way down her torso, tasting her skin like fine wine. Every part of her tastes like home. And when I reach her core, I pause, taking a deep breath to inhale the scent that fills my senses. She's aroused, wet, and ready for me. She gasps when I dip my tongue inside her pussy, tasting her sweetness. For a moment, she's mine once more.

I spread her legs wider, holding her hips steady as I take her completely into my mouth, my tongue dancing against her sensitive pussy. Her cries echo through the darkness, and I can't help but groan in response. She tastes like heaven, and I'm lost in the moment, devouring her like she's the last meal I'll ever have. My cock throbs, aching for release, but I want her to come first.

I work her slowly, teasingly, sending waves of pleasure coursing through her body. She's squirming beneath me, arching her back, wanting more. And when she does, I give it to her—my tongue circling and flicking against her clit until she screams my name. Her juices coat my mouth, and I drink greedily, savoring the taste of her as her legs quiver at my touch.

Finally, she's sated, panting heavily. And as she lies there, spent, I climb onto the blanket and position myself between her legs. She watches me with a hungry look in her eyes, a combination of fear and desire that sends shivers down my spine. "Take me hard," she whispers.

I oblige, sliding my rock hard cock slowly into her tight heat. She's hot and wet, surrounding me completely. Her nails dig into my shoulders as I thrust into her, our hips slapping together in a rhythm that echoes off the buildings surrounding us. We're a symphony of lust—a duet of grunts and moans that fill the night air.

And then, we both reach our climaxes at once, her body shuddering violently beneath me as I pour my seed into her. We collapse, sweaty and satisfied, tangled together under the starry sky.

I pull her closer, holding her against my chest. Her head rests over my heart, rising and falling with each breath.

We lie there in silence for a while, basking in the afterglow, the stars twinkling overhead. Despite the chill in the air, warmth floods my body—a deep contentment I've never known before her.

"What now?" she asks softly, tracing circles on my chest with her finger.

"Now, we build our future," I reply. "Together."

It won't be easy. There are still those who would see us torn apart, who resent our union and the changes it brings. But they don't understand what we have. An unbreakable bond forged in history, fire and blood. A love that transcends reason and defies all odds.

As long as we stand united, no one can stand against us. I know there will be challenges ahead, obstacles we must overcome. But I have faith in us. In the end, our love will prevail.

I tilt her chin up and kiss her deeply, filled with hope and purpose. Our future is about to change, shaped by our vision of what it could be. A future of peace and prosperity, not corruption and violence.

When we part, I smile down at her. "Ready to take on the world, tesoro?"

She smiles back, eyes glinting with determination. "As long as I have you by my side."

Together, we leave the rooftop and return to the villa—originally mine and now very much ours—ready to face whatever comes our way.

Sixteen

Alessia

The slamming of the door jolts me awake. I sit up in bed, heart racing, as Marco strides into the room. His shoulders are tense, his jaw clenched. It's clear that our escape from our old lives has taken its toll.

"Another nightmare?" I ask softly.

Marco nods, raking a hand through his disheveled hair. "I can't stop seeing their faces. Everyone who died for us."

I slide over, patting the space beside me. Marco hesitates before sitting down on the edge of the mattress.

"It wasn't your fault," I murmur.

"Yes, it was. I put everyone in danger by defying my father." Marco's voice cracks. "And now they're gone. I still can't believe Rocco is gone. Any of them."

My chest aches at his pain. I know what it's like to carry the weight of the dead. Gently, I take his hand in mine.

"We've both lost so much. But we still have each other." I squeeze his hand. "I'm here for you, Marco. Whatever comes next, we'll face it together."

Marco turns, his dark eyes glistening. "I don't deserve you, Alessia."

"Yes, you absolutely do." I cup his cheek. "You're a great man trying to break free from a cruel world that you never entered into by choice. I believe in the life we can build, without violence, without fear."

Marco presses his forehead to mine. "You give me hope," he whispers.

We stay like that for a long moment, drawing strength from each other. The past can't be changed, but the future is ours to shape. As long as Marco and I are together, I know we'll be okay. The long night is over. Dawn has finally come.

Marco and I settle into our new life, far removed from the dangers of his father's criminal empire. Here in this sleepy seaside town, we can finally breathe easy.

Our modest cottage by the cliffs is simple but cozy. Marco seems lighter, smiling more as he putters around the garden or cooks dinner in our tiny kitchen. At night, we curl up together on the porch swing, listening to the steady crash of waves.

After so many years of living on edge, the quiet takes some getting used to. But I cherish these private moments with Marco, talking and laughing late into the evening. We speak of small things, our hopes rather than our fears.

There are still shadows, of course. I catch Marco staring off into the distance, sadness creeping across his face. And my own nightmares persist, visions of blood and gunfire jolting me awake. But we are healing, day by day.

On our long walks along the beach, Marco squeezes my hand gratefully. "Thank you for this life," he says. I smile up at him. "We built this together."

Our scars may never fully fade, but we wear them with pride now. They are marks of what we have survived and overcome. Marco and I still have each other. That's all that matters.

Marco

My departure sent shockwaves through the underworld I once dominated. For years, my iron grip kept rival families and factions in check. But now, the balance of power has been thrown into chaos.

I dream about the fallout. I'm sure that in the ornate halls of the Bertolini estate, Enzo seethes as he paces back and forth. Formerly one of my most trusted advisors, I'm sure he assumed he would inherit control. But those above us had other plans, refusing to name Enzo as successor, and instead naming Luca who has remained loyal and consistent over all the years we've worked together.

"That bastard abandoned us!" I imagine Enzo snarling, hurling his glass at the wall. "The family stood by him through everything. And how does he repay us?"

I picture the don sitting stoically behind his massive desk, defending my decision. "Marco made his choice. We must look forward now."

But if I know anything about my cousin, it's that Enzo will not let go so easily. He still has loyalists on his side, men as angry and bitter as he is. Enzo's lust for power knows no bounds. If the don won't give him control, he'll be prepared to take it by force.

In the coming weeks, tensions escalate. Suspicious accidents befall those loyal to the don. Strong-arm tactics intimidate rivals into submission. The family teeters on the brink of civil war.

And from the shadows, the wolves circle. The Gallos and Zitos see opportunity in the chaos, moving to claim my syndicate's old territory. Bloody skirmishes erupt as they test the waters.

Sitting on my porch late one night, I feel the pull of my old life. I cannot stand by while my family self-destructs. But the choice has been made. This quiet life with Alessia is all that matters now. As difficult as it is to watch from a distance, the darkness will have to fight on without me.

Alessia

The morning sun streams into our new bedroom, stirring me from sleep. I stretch and revel in the simple luxury of waking up next to Marco, no alarms or obligations rushing us. We have all the time in the world now.

Marco stirs beside me, his arm draped loosely over my waist. His eyes blink open and he smiles.

"Good morning, my love," he says, his voice still husky with sleep.

"Good morning," I reply, snuggling into his chest.

We lie together in comfortable silence, hands idly caressing each other's skin. No words need to be said. The peace between us is palpable.

Eventually Marco sighs, "I suppose we should start planning our day."

I prop myself up on one elbow. "We could look at some of those brochures your real estate agent left. Pick out a nice little house with a big backyard."

Marco grins. "As long as it has a master bedroom fit for a king and queen."

I swat his chest playfully. "Is that all you think about?"

"With you lying here looking like that? Absolutely." His eyes smolder as he pulls me in for a long, deep kiss.

When we finally break apart, breathless, I say, "Well, a king-sized bed is non-negotiable. But I also want space for an art studio."

Marco nods. "Of course. And plenty of room to grow our own vegetables."

My heart swells thinking of the simple life we'll build together. No more looking over our shoulders, no more violence. Just peace, and love, and each other.

I take a deep breath as I stare at my reflection in the full-length mirror. The simple white gown flows gracefully over my body, the lace sleeves just barely brushing my wrists. My hair is pinned back in a delicate twist, a few curled tendrils framing my face.

It's hard to believe this day has finally arrived. After everything Marco and I endured, all the pain and heartache, we've made it here. To our wedding day.

A knock at the door startles me from my thoughts. Marco's sister, Gioia, pokes her head in. "It's time," she says softly.

I nod, blinking back sudden tears. Gioia comes over and gives me a careful hug. "You look beautiful. Marco is a lucky man."

"Thank you," I whisper. Arm in arm, we walk down the hall towards the backyard.

The sun is just beginning to set over the vineyard, bathing everything in a warm golden glow. White chairs are set up on either side of a simple wooden arbor, woven through with vines and white roses. Candles flicker gently.

My breath catches as I see Marco standing tall and proud beneath the arbor, hands clasped behind his back. His black suit fits him like a glove, the white shirt crisp against his tan skin. Our eyes meet and everything else fades away.

Gioia kisses my cheek. "Go get him," she urges. I blink back more tears and begin the slow walk towards my future husband.

Towards the man who fought through hell with me. Who chose me above all else. The man I will give my whole heart to, for the rest of my days.

With tears in both of our eyes, I link arms with my Nonna Giulia, the woman who taught me everything I know and sheltered me from the dark secrets that ultimately led me to today. There is nobody else I could have wished to give me away.

As I reach him, Marco extends his hand. I place mine in his strong grip.

"You look exquisite, my love," he murmurs.

"As do you," I whisper back.

The minister begins speaking but I hardly hear the words. Marco and I are lost in each other's gaze, fingers entwined, souls knitted together.

Finally it's time for the vows. Marco clears his throat and begins.

"Alessia, my light in the darkness. From the moment I met you, my entire world shifted..."

Marco's voice is thick with emotion as he continues his vows:

"You saw beyond the shadows of my past and found the man I longed to be. Your spirit, your courage, your unwavering heart - they fueled me, guided me, as I broke free from the chains that bound me.

You make me laugh without even trying. You get me on a level that nobody else does. When I dreamed of my match—the one who I could truly call my soulmate, it seemed out of my grasp. But then you came into my life and that all changed. Now, I can't imagine a cell in my body existing without you being near. You fill me with life, with a happiness and joy that I thought was left behind in childhood. You are my everything, and I'm so excited to spend the rest of my life with you.

Now, I pledge myself to you fully and completely. I will cherish each moment we have together. I will stand by your side through all life brings our way. I will honor, protect, and nurture the rare, precious gift of your love.

You are my redemption, my salvation. Today I join my life with yours, and take my first steps into a beautiful new world. A world we will build, side by side, with patience, compassion and joy."

Tears blur my vision as I begin my vows to Marco.

"My darling, when I first met you I saw a good man trapped in darkness. My heart broke for the pain you endured, but I also saw your strength, your spirit, your capacity for love and loyalty.

You've proven yourself to be the man I always knew you were inside. As we start our new life together, I vow to be your soft place to land when the world seems harsh. I vow to share in your hopes and dreams, and help you achieve them. I vow to nurture our bond, and the family we will grow. And I will be strong for you, and for our family.

You've given me the greatest gift—the freedom to be my true self. With you I have found a home. And I pledge to make our home one of peace, understanding and devotion.

I love you with everything that I am. I can't wait to experience all that our future holds, with you by my side."

As we exchange rings, our eyes glisten. We speak the final binding words in unison, voices choked with joy.

"With this ring, I thee wed."

His lips find mine, soft yet demanding. His hands hold onto mine, the warmth of our rings seeping into my flesh. Our tongues dance, and I feel his passion, his love, his need. We are one.

The reception room and its rowdy festivities disappear as we make our way to our wedding suite, the door shutting with a soft click behind us. The bed is massive, fit for a king and queen, but it's not the size that steals my breath, it's the anticipation of what will happen on it. I've never felt this way with anyone. It's as if Marco and I are two magnets, gravitating towards each other. Our souls intertwined.

He undresses me slowly, his eyes devouring every inch of my exposed skin. I gasp at the sensation. He's gentle when he takes off my dress, reverential as he lays it on a chair. I watch him undress, my heart beating wildly in my chest. His muscles ripple as he sheds his tuxedo, revealing a body honed by years of work and discipline. His abs ripple, and I admire the trail of his obliques that create two firm lines descending directly toward his cock like two helpful signposts.

He pulls me onto the bed, and we tangle together, our bodies intertwining. He kisses my neck, his stubble grazing my skin, sending shivers down my spine. "Alessia," he whispers in my ear, his voice rough with desire.

Our hands explore each other's bodies, mapping out new territories. He finds my most sensitive spots, tracing circles around my nipples with his thumbs, making me moan softly. I arch into him, needing more. He chuckles darkly, the sound sending a shiver down my spine. In one swift move, he enters me. We both gasp at the sensation, his cock dragging against my walls. I dig my nails into his back as he begins to move.

The pace is slow and sensual. We have all the time in the world to explore each other. Marco kisses me deeply, his tongue tangling with mine. I meet his thrusts, our bodies moving as one. The pleasure builds and builds, like waves lapping at the shore.

"Alessia, my wife," Marco groans. "You feel so good."

His words send a spike of pleasure through me. I trail kisses down his neck, tasting his salty skin. He shudders, his movements becoming more urgent. I move my hips to meet his, chasing my release.

When it hits me, it's like nothing I've experienced before. My back arches and I cry out Marco's name. He follows soon after, burying his face in my neck.

We stay like that for a long time, our heartbeats slowing. I run my fingers through his hair. Marco lifts his head and smiles at me, a smile full of love and tenderness.

"Thank you for marrying me, Alessia," he says softly.

I cup his cheek. "There's nowhere else I'd rather be than here with you, Marco."

He kisses me again, slow and sweet. And in this moment, I know that we've finally found our happy ending.

We lie in each other's arms, basking in the afterglow. So much has changed since Marco first brought me into his world. I went from being an oblivious pawn in some mysterious game to finding love in the unlikeliest of places.

Marco strokes my hair. "Do you regret any of it, my queen?"

I shake my head. "Not for a second. Every struggle we went through brought me closer to you. I'd go through it all again if it meant ending up here."

"I never thought I'd find someone who could bring light to my dark world," Marco says. "You were the missing piece of me I didn't know was missing until I found you."

Tears prick my eyes at his words. "You gave me a home when I had none. A place where I could be myself without fear of judgment." I look up at him, smiling through my tears. "Together, we defeated the darkness."

Marco kisses the top of my head. "And together, we'll build a future filled with light."

The challenges ahead loom, but they don't frighten me. As long as Marco and I stand united, there is no obstacle we can't overcome. We've already triumphed over forces that sought to keep us apart. A happy future is ours for the taking.

I snuggle closer to Marco, secure in the knowledge that I'm exactly where I'm meant to be. Our story may have started in darkness, in confusion, in fear. But that's not how it ends. Because together, Marco and I have found our light.

The next morning, Marco and I stand outside the little house we've purchased. It's small but cozy, with a garden filled with lavender bushes and a little stone path leading to the front door. I'd always considered myself a city girl, but Marco has helped me to realize many new things about myself.

"Ready to continue our new adventure?" Marco asks, smiling down at me.

I lace my fingers through his and squeeze his hand. "As long as I'm with you, I'm ready for anything."

We walk up the path together, the gravel crunching under our shoes. Marco unlocks the front door and sweeps me into his arms before carrying me over the threshold.

I laugh, smacking his chest playfully. "Put me down, you brute!"

"Never. I'm going to carry you everywhere for the rest of our lives." His eyes gleam with mirth and love as he kicks the front door closed behind us.

He sets me on my feet in the foyer, pulling me close for a deep, passionate kiss. When we break apart, I'm breathless.

Marco strokes my cheek, gazing at me with a tenderness that makes my heart ache. "Welcome home, Mrs. Moretti-De Luca."

"Welcome home," I echo, realizing this little house represents so much more than four walls and a roof.

It's a sanctuary. A place to reset and start over, to create a future as bright as the love Marco and I share.

Our struggles have ended, and our new adventure is just beginning.

Blood and Sand (Dark Reverse Harem Mafia Romance)

- Sea of Snakes(Book 1)

- Sea of Sinners(Book 2)

- Sea of Rage (Book 3)

- Sea of Pain(Book 4)

- Sinners, Rage & Pain: The Brixton Trilogy(Books 2, 3 and 4)

- Sea of Demons(Book 5)

- Sea of Redemption(Book 6)

Palm Falls Series (mafia romance – interconnected standalones)

- F*CKBOYS

- Bronson & Wren's story (title TBC)

Standalones

- Rucked (sports romance – RH/why choose)

- Ruthless Choices(romantic horror)

Billionaire's Takeover Collection

- Irreversible Decision

- Compelling Proposal

- Love Merger

- The Billionaire's Takeover Collection (all 3 of the above!)

Novellas

- Love in a Seedy Motel Room

Sign up for my newsletter herefor the latest on new releases, promos, giveaways and events!

Join me on social media:
Facebook: @heidistarkauthor
Instagram: @heiditstarkauthor
TikTok: @heidistark_author
Twitter: @heidistarkauthr

Websitehttps://heidistarkauthor.com

Heidi Stark is an indie dark romance author who grew up in New Zealand and now resides in the US.

She is inspired by the locations she visits on her travels, and the people she meets along the way.

When she's not writing, you can usually find her reading, listening to podcasts, or dreaming about her next book.

Learn more about Heidi Stark at her website. Sign up for exclusive content and her newsletter here.

You can also find out more about Heidi and her upcoming books on social media:

Facebook Page

Facebook Group

Instagram

TikTok

Made in the USA
Las Vegas, NV
31 March 2024

88067316R00121